KB242778

A Cognitive Linguistic Approach to English Idioms

From a Pedagogical Perspective

A Cognitive Linguistic Approach to English Idioms

From a Pedagogical Perspective

◆ 박 경 선 지음 ◆

KSI 한국학술정보㈜

Acknowledgements

This thesis has greatly benefitted from comments, suggestions and discussions of the members of my dissertation committee, Professors Jae-Young Joh, Sung-Yun Bak, Hang-Jin Yoon, Seongha Rhee and Jeong-Woon Park. I express sincere appreciation to Professors Jae-Young Joh and Sung-Yun Bak, who showed interest in this dissertation and gave many valuable suggestions. My special thanks should also go to Professor Hang-Jin Yoon for his detailed corrections and insightful comments. I also like to thank Professor Seongha Rhee for his insightful criticisms and suggestions. Above all, I owe a debt of gratitude to my advisor, Professor Jeong-Woon Park, who guided me into the field of cognitive linguistics and made crucial contributions to this dissertation. He was always ready to meet with me and gave me many valuable suggestions and detailed comments in every page of this dissertation.

I would like to express my deep gratitude to the late Professor In-Seok Yang, who led me into the field of linguistics and guided and encouraged me throughout my graduate study. I am also indebted to Professors Soon-Ham Park, Kook Chung, Sun-Woo Lee, Kyu-Se Shim and Dong-Il Lee for their kind guidance and teaching.

My final thanks belong to my family. My parents always gave me encouragement and support enough to finish this dissertation. My mother-in-law took care of her three grandsons. My husband, Dr. Dong-Soon Kim, and my three sons, Young-Do, Hyun-Do and Sun-Do, patiently put up with all too much inconvenience without any complaints. Without their love and support, I could not have completed this thesis.

TABLE OF CONTENTS

CHAPTER 1

Introduction

1. Purpose and Framework

This dissertation is an analysis of idioms from the framework of cognitive linguistics. Many idioms, if not all, are systematically motivated by various conceptual metaphors and metonymies whose research helps to find out an effective methodology in educating English idioms to Korean speakers.

Idioms are used in our everyday lives, and they are vivid and memorable representations of a situation or a behavior. People think that idioms are easier to remember than the corresponding "normal" expressions. Native speakers learn and use idioms in an easy and natural way, while non-native speakers or second-language learners have difficulty in learning and using them because they don't know the context or the convention within which idioms have been used.

Usually the meaning of an idiom differs from that of the simple combination of each word participating in the idiom. Idioms differ in their idiomaticity and they do not constitute a homogeneous category. They appear to be unsystematic and inexplicable.

In the framework of formal grammar, idioms have been studied on the basis of their syntactic properties. As for the semantic properties of idioms, the meanings of idioms are considered to be non-compositional and arbitrary, so that idioms must enter the lexicon as complete phrases.

With the development of cognitive linguistics which centers on human cognitive processes and meaning, it is noted that the syntactic behaviors of idioms are associated with their semantic and pragmatic properties, and that idioms constitute a continuum scale from the pole of compositionality to that of non-compositionality. Non-compositional idioms such as *kick the bucket* are recognized as one word and allow no syntactic transformation, whereas compositional ones such as *lay down the law* allow such transformations as the passive and the components of idioms contribute to the overall figurative meanings. Many idioms are also in the middle on the continuum of analyzability. Some of them approach non-compositional idioms, and others are near compositional ones. The more analyzable an idiom is, the more syntactically productive it is. Therefore, the syntactic behaviors of idioms are not arbitrary and the syntactic versatility of idioms can be explained by their internal semantics and convention, which means the syntactic productivity of idioms depends to a large extent on their semantic properties.

Some cognitive linguists like Glucksberg (1993) admit diversity among idioms. That is to say, idioms differ in the degree of lexical substitutions, syntactic operations, and semantic productivity. In general, the more compositional an idiom is, the more variation it has, although compositionality alone is insufficient to restrict the idiom use. Even in seemingly unanalyzable idioms such as *by and large*, linguistic meaning plays an important role. Thus, Glucksberg concludes that listeners understand speakers' intention uniting literal meaning, stipulated-idiomatic meaning, and allusional meaning according to discourse contexts.

The figurative meanings of idioms, in many cases, are motivated by various conceptual metaphors that underlie as a part of our conceptual system. People may understand idioms by mapping from the "source domain" to the "target domain." For example, when English speakers understand *John let off steams* to mean "John got angry," they recognize *anger* in terms of "heat" or "internal pressure" because they have conceptual metaphors such as ANGER IS HEAT, MIND IS A CONTAINER and EMOTIONAL STATES ARE ENTITIES (cf. Lakoff 1987). The conceptual metaphors on which our experience is grounded help us to understand *let off steam* as "release tension from anger." In other words, people tend to understand abstract ideas or conceptual domains in terms of concrete domains. According to Gibbs and O'Brien (1990), people have tacit knowledge of the metaphorical basis and strong conventional images for many idioms. In their experiment, people showed high consistency in their images of idioms with similar figurative meanings despite differences in their surface forms.

This study aims to explore how idioms are systematically motivated by various conceptual metaphors and metonymies, and to explain

English idioms in the framework of cognitive linguistics. Especially, it explores how metaphors or metonymies involved in idioms are related to their overall figurative meanings through the case study of some color term idioms and some body-part term idioms motivated by various metaphors and metonymies.

This study also aims to contribute to some pedagogical purposes. Most Korean students learning English consider English idioms to be very difficult to understand and they rarely use them in their speaking or writing. The cognitive analysis of idioms can help English learners to understand and learn them easily. In other words, the explanation about the basic conceptual metaphors in English may help Korean students to learn and understand English idioms.

This study is made up of five chapters. Section 1.2 examines various definitions of idioms which have been proposed in the literature. Chapter 2 discusses some aspects of cognitive linguistics. It surveys the classical theory of categorization and the prototype theory, and examines the types of idioms proposed in the literature. It also examines the properties of metaphor and metonymy, and proposes that conceptual metaphors or metonymies underlie many idioms.

Chapter 3 pursues a cognitive linguistic explanation of idioms. Especially, conceptual metaphors and metonymies are explicated which a large number of color term and body-part term idioms are based on. Also, English and Korean idioms in such domains are compared with regard to their similarities and differences.

Chapter 4 deals with the issue of idiom comprehensions which is based on an experiment on how non-native speakers understand and learn English idioms. Subjects were all native Korean speakers who have been learning English as a foreign language. Through the experiment I explore in which respects non-native speakers have something in common with native speakers in understanding in English idioms, and how much influence the conceptual metaphors and metonymies in their own native language as well as the context make on the comprehension of idioms. The results of the experiment show that the explanation about the basic conceptual metaphors in English help Korean students to learn and understand English idioms more easily.

Chapter 5 is a brief summary of this study. What is more important in this study is to illustrate, on the basis of the cognitive research on idioms, that many idioms are motivated by some conceptual metaphors and metonymies and they can be explained in some generalized way.

2. Definitions of Idioms

Traditionally an idiom is considered to consist of more than one word and its meaning cannot be inferred from the meaning of each word of the idiom. In other words, the usual semantic rules for combining meanings do not apply to the idioms.

Chafe (1968: 111) mentions the importance of idioms in language, and argues that the present Chomskyan framework cannot explain idioms naturally and convincingly. He refers to four peculiarities of idioms—anomalous meaning, transformational deficiency, ill-formedness and the greater text frequency. The first peculiarity, anomalous meaning means that the meaning of an idiom is not amalgamation of the meanings of the parts of the structure. Rather, the meaning of an idiom is comparable to the meaning of a single lexical item. For instance, the meaning of *kick the bucket* is not made up of the meanings associated with "kick," "the" and "bucket," but it simply denotes the meaning of 'die.' Transformation deficiency mentions that most, if not all, idioms are not applied by transformations such as passivization, nominalization, etc. without changing their meanings. That is to say, idioms may or may not undergo transformations, but they generally lose idiomatic meaning after the application of transformations. For example, *Tom kicked the bucket* means 'Tom died,' but *The bucket was kicked by Tom* cannot have the idiomatic meaning. Ill-formedness refers to the fact that there are some idioms which are not syntactically well-formed. *By* and *large* and *trip the light fantastic* are such examples. The greater text frequency means that an idiom is used more frequently than its literal counterpart. In other words, the expression, *kick the bucket,* means 'to die' more often than it means 'to strike the pail with one's foot.'

Fraser (1970) regards idioms not as the combination of parts but as a single unit. He proposes that idioms do not constitute a homogeneous class on transformations, which he calls "Frozenness Hierarchy." His hierarchy consists of seven classes, and the classes differ in permitting some transformations by degrees. It means that he also admits idioms are not explained in a binary way.

Longman Dictionary of English Idioms (1979) refers to two kinds of idioms. First, an idiom is a phrase which means something different from the combined meaning of each word in the phrase. Second, an idiom is a typical style of a person or a group of people in his / their use of language. In this dissertation I use the term *idiom* in the sense of the first definition. The dictionary also mentions the characteristics of idioms. First, the expressions are metaphorical rather than literal. Because they are metaphorical, one cannot usually discover their meanings by looking up individual words in an ordinary dictionary. Second, they are also more or less invariable or fixed in form or order in a way that makes them different from literal expressions. Because they are more or less invariable, they cannot be changed or varied in the way literal expressions are normally varied. Although metaphorical meaning and invariability are the characteristics of idioms, they vary a great deal in how metaphorical or invariable they are. In other words, idiomaticity is a matter of degree or scale. Third, most of them are phrases of two or more words. Finally, many of these expressions belong to informal spoken English rather than to formal written English.

Nunberg, Ivan and Wasow (1994: 492) suggest that idiomaticity generally implies conventionality, inflexibility, figuration, proverbiality, informality, and affect. "Conventionality" means that idioms are conventionalized. "Inflexibility" denotes that idioms appear in the limited number of syntactic frames or constructions. As for figuration, idioms are supposed to include figurations such as metaphors, meto-nymies, and hyperboles. *Take the bull by the horns* is an example of metaphor whereas *lend a hand* and *count heads* are examples of metonymy; *not worth the paper it's printed on* is an example of hyperboles. What proverbiality means is that idioms are used to describe situations of social concern. Informality means that idioms are generally associated with informal or colloquial speech. Affect means that idioms imply a certain evaluation or affective stance toward the things they denote. Except for conventionality, the other properties are not always applied to all idioms, but idiomaticity weakens as a phrase lacks some of these properties. They propose that idioms are situational metaphors and that the existence of idiom families reputes the standard view of idioms of the formal grammar. That is, the same NP is often used with two or more idiomatic verbs: *Keep / lose / blow one's cool, keep / start / have the ball rolling*, etc.

Therefore, they propose to distinguish idiomatically combining expressions from idiomatic phrases. The meanings of idiomatically combining expressions are distributed among their parts, so that it may be called compositional. Examples are *take advantage of* and *pull strings*. Idiomatically combining expressions include not only the idioms whose meanings can be predicted on the basis of a know-ledge of the meanings of their parts but also the idioms whose meanings can be predicted from the contexts. *Pull strings* is the latter case, and it means something like 'exploit personal connections.' If we hear it in isolation, we may not predict its meaning. But from the sentence, *John was able to pull strings to get the job, since he had a lot of contacts in the industry* (Nunberg et al. 1994: 496), we will be able to establish correspondences between *pull* and *exploit*, and between *strings* and *connections*. In this case, each constituent of the idiom refers metaphorically to a part of the interpretation.

Idiomatic phrases do not distribute the interpretation into the individual parts, so that they can enter the lexicon as complete phrases. Most syntactic operations change the idiomatic interpretation. Examples are *kick the bucket, shoot the breeze, saw logs*, etc. The class of idiomatic phrases is smaller than that of idiomatically combining expressions. They also maintain that the syntactic behavior of idioms is not arbitrary, so that the semantic properties of idioms and the metaphors that many of them employ may help to explain their syntactic behavior. One instance is that the more analyzable an idiom is, the more syntactically productive it is.

I propose that idioms differ in conventionality, transparency and compositionality, and they are related to one another. If the mapping from the individual components to the idiomatic referents is transparent and conventional, it is the case of normally decomposable idioms (cf. Gibbs & Nayak 1989). Let's take some examples, *lay down the law* and *pop the question. Lay down* means the act of invoking the law, and *the law* refers to laws or rules. In the case of the latter, the concept of "popping" is related to that of "suddenly asking" or "proposing." The concept of "the question" is associated with that of "proposal" or "marriage." That is, the individual parts of *pop the question* are all in the same conceptual domain or in the same semantic field.

Abnormally decomposable idioms have metaphorical relations between the components and the referents. Accordingly, the mapping of these idioms is less transparent and less conventional than that of normally decomposable idioms, and they are difficult to change syntactically. For example, *spill the beans* is abnormally decomposable. *Spill* has the concept of "revealing" or "exposing of," but *beans* are indirectly or opaquely associated with the concept of "secret." So, only some parts of the idiom are in the same conceptual domain.

No part of non-decomposable idioms such as *shoot the breeze* has the same conceptual domain as "to talk without purpose." That is, the individual components do not contribute to the overall figurative meaning, so it is semantically non-decomposable. Therefore, idioms have motivation, but no regularity, and their symbolization processes are not entirely arbitrary but culturally bound.

Idioms have some general properties, but they are not always required, which may make idioms constitute a heterogeneous class and a continuum scale. The prototype theory helps to explain their behavior.

CHAPTER 2

Some Aspects
of Cognitive Linguistics

Language is one of the obvious means to represent human thoughts. Cognitive linguistics looks upon language from the point of conception and thoughts. That is to say, it regards language as a part of cognitive systems including perception, emotion, categorization, inferences, etc.

This chapter examines some aspects of cognitive linguistics. In section 2.1, I will review the prototype theory in comparison with the classical theory and explore types of idioms on the basis of the prototype theory. In section 2.2, I will review the theories and properties of metaphor and metonymy.

1. The Prototype Theory

Traditionally, idioms have been considered to be non-compositional. That is, the meaning of each constituent word in an idiom does not contribute to that of the idiom. But idiomaticity must not be identified with non-compositionality, and idioms constitute a continuum as seen in section 1.2. The prototype theory helps us to understand the behavior of idioms.

1) The Prototype Theory and the Classical Theory

Since Aristotle's classical theory of categorization, we have been familiar with the binary categorization. The assumptions of the classical theory are as follows: First, categories are defined in terms of a conjunction of necessary and sufficient features, so all members of a category have shared properties. Even if a thing lacks only one of the necessary and sufficient features of a category, it cannot be a member of the category. Second, features are binary, which means features are a matter of all or nothing, so that they can have only the [+] or [−] value. Third, categories have clear boundaries, which implies there are no borderline cases and there is no fuzziness. Fourth, all members of a category have equal status. That is, there are no degrees of membership in a category. Fifth, category boundaries are not flexible, so that human purposes or context cannot change the boundary. Sixth, all the psychological factors are excluded. The world is made up of objects with fixed relations among themselves.

Such an Aristotelian categorization model has made much influence on linguistics in the 20th century. Linguists usually divide language into two parts. For example, Saussure separates synchronic linguistics from diachronic linguistics, and langue from parole. Chomsky distinguishes language competence from performance. The generative phonology presented in Chomsky and Halle (1968) uses binary distinctive features.[1] People have become used to dividing things into two parts.

Wittgenstein (1958) refers to the definition of *Spiel* 'game.' He notes that various members of the game category do not share the common properties, but they constitute a chain of similarities or a complex network of similarities. He calls these similarities "family resemblances," for several members of a family have various resemblances—color of eyes, temperament, build, features, etc. And he mentions that the category is learned on the basis of exemplars, which is the same concept as prototype.

Labov (1973) testifies the insights of Wittgenstein with some experiments on household receptacles such as cups, mugs, bowls and vases. He showed several receptacles with various shapes to the subjects, who were asked to categorize them into cups, mugs, bowls and vases. The experiment shows that there is no distinct boundary between cup and bowl, and the contents like coffee, potatoes, or flowers make an effect on the concept of the category. That is, even

---

1) Recently the Optimality Theory in phonology selects the optimal form in terms of the rankings of constraints, where degree is the most important concept. Cf. Prince & Smolensky (1993).

the same receptacle might be categorized differently according to whether it is used for drinking coffee or for eating mashed potatoes. Attributes of cups, bowls, and vases include the characteristic shape, size, and material of the receptacle. No single attribute can distinguish two categories, but only increases the possibility of categorization. The attributes are not concerned with intrinsic properties of the object itself, but with the role of the object within a particular culture. There is a certain optimum value for the width−depth ratio of each receptacle, which is the prototype. In categorizing an entity, we should consider how closely the dimensions of the entity approximate to the optimum dimensions.

Rosch (1975) investigates the structure of natural categories through experiments. The subjects were asked to judge to what extent certain kinds of household items could be regarded as good examples of furniture. 60 household items made a continuum of goodness-of-example, among which chair and sofa are the prototypical members and telephone is the peripheral member of furniture. If people are asked to name exemplars of a category, they tend to mention the more prototypical members first; thus, the membership degree of a category is the reflection of a psychologically real concept.

The prototype representations of many categories change over time and space. The prototypical cars of fifty years ago are now marginal examples of the categories. In the experiment to German-speaking subjects, they think that a bed and a table are the typical examples of furniture (cf. Table 3.2 in Taylor 1995: 57). But English-speaking subjects think that chair and sofa are the typical examples of furniture. Prototype splits show the historic development of prototype category.

Ungerer and Schmid (1996: 266) present the prototype change of the category IDEA.

(a) IDEA =CONCEPT, MENTAL PICTURE
 The idea of truth is hard to grasp.
(b) IDEA =BELIEF
 The idea that the earth is a disc.
(c) IDEA =AIM, PLAN
 The idea is to put all cards.
(d) IDEA =SUDDEN INSPIRATION
 And then he had a brilliant idea.

(a) 1430－1770   (b) 1770－1830   (c) after 1830

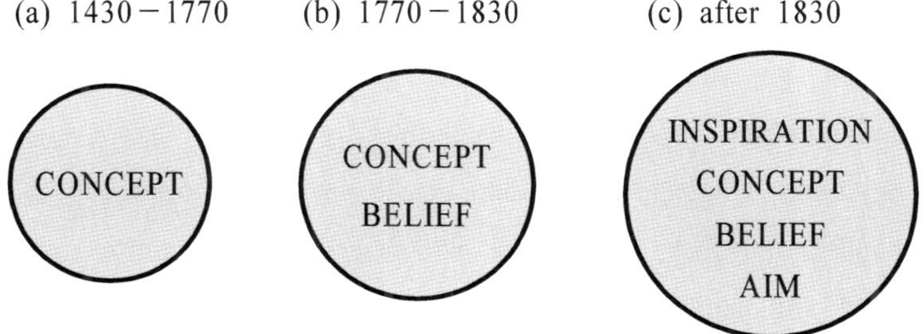

Prototypical members of a cognitive category share most of the attributes of the category with other members, and share almost no attributes with the members of other categories. Peripheral members of a category share some attributes with other members of the category, and have a few attributes of other categories. Thus, the boundary of a category is fuzzy. The membership of a category is given by resemblances with other members including prototypes. The more closely an object approaches the prototype, the more central it becomes in the category. But similarity is a subjective psychological concept. This is one of the problems of the prototype theory. It does not have an absolute criterion in ranking members. In other words, the distance between prototypical members and peripheral members is not absolute but relative, so that it is difficult to decide the degree of typicalness within a category. How many differences make things not similar? The cognitive linguistics is concerned with the following psychological entities rather than physical objects: how things are perceived, how people interact with objects, what people's intentions are, and what their mental images are.

The basic level categorization also shows that the classical categorization theory is false. According to Lakoff (1982: 146), in the American sign language, basic level categories are represented by single signs and superordinate categories by multiple sign sequences. In children's language acquisition, basic level categories are named and understood first. Basic level categories have the shortest primary lexemes, and subjects are fastest in identifying category members at the level. Take a category DOG for instance. The category DOG has subcategories, RETRIEVER, TERRIER, HOUND, etc., while it has the superordinate concept, MAMMAL. Words of the basic level represent the property of the category best, because superordinate level has obscure properties and subordinate level lacks generality because of its specificity. The classical theory of categorization cannot admit the existence of basic level category because the members have equal status in membership.

Another piece of evidence that the classical theory is false comes from hedge expressions, which represent the degree of the membership in a category. *Par excellence* has a function of selecting central members of a category, so that it restructures the category with prototypical or near-prototypical members.

(1) A robin is a bird par excellence.
(2) ?A chicken is a bird par excellence.

Loosely speaking restructures and enlarges the category by excluding central members.

(3) ?Loosely speaking, a chair is a piece of furniture.
(4) Loosely speaking, a telephone is a piece of furniture.

Strictly speaking also excludes central members but it removes ambiguity on the boundary.

(5) A whale is a fish. (false)
(6) Strictly speaking, a whale is a fish. (false)
(7) Loosely speaking, a whale is a fish.
    (true or at least not patently false)
(8) Loosely speaking, a whale is a fish in that it swims and
    lives in the sea. (better)

The hedges make us distinguish central members from peripheral ones, and distinguish degrees of non-members. They show that the category boundaries are flexible, so that they show that the classical theory is false.

The prototype concept is also applied to the linguistic categories as well as the conceptual categories. Just as there are central and peripheral members of the conceptual categories BIRD, FURNITURE and FISH, so the linguistic categories NOUN, VERB, etc. have representative and marginal members. In other words, the prototype effects permeate the structure of language.

Bybee and Moder (1983: 267) suggest that "the psychological principles which govern linguistic behavior are the same as those which govern other types of human behavior." They study certain morphological alternations in English. English strong verbs include *sing*, which shows the vowel alternation $/ɪ/ - /æ/ - /ʌ/$ in the present tense, past tense, and past participle, and *cling*, which has the pattern $/ɪ/ - /ʌ/ - /ʌ/$ This class has been productive enough to extend to other verbs like *ring, fling, stick* and *dig*. In addition, verbs with a vowel other than $/ɪ/$ in the present tense such as *hang* and *strike* have been added to the class. The prototypical members of the class are *sing* and *cling*, which have a velar nasal as the final consonant of the stem. Some peripheral members have a non-velar nasal like *swim, win* and *spin* and other peripheral members such as *stick* and *dig* ending in a non-nasal velar. Table 1 shows that only *sing* and *cling* satisfy three conditions, and each member satisfies different conditions. However, not only *sing* and *cling* but also others are the members of the same class of English strong verbs. This means that the claim of the classical theory that all members of a category have shared properties is false.

Table 1. Properties of English strong verbs

(cf. Taylor 1995: 175)

	/ɪ/ in present tense	Velar as final consonant	Nasal as final consonant
sing	yes	yes	yes
cling	yes	yes	yes
hang	no	yes	yes
swim	yes	no	yes
stick	yes	yes	no
strike	no	yes	no

2) Types of Idioms based on the Prototype Theory

Idioms have syntactic and semantic properties. The formal syntacticians put an emphasis on syntactic operations. Chafe (1968: 111) suggests that idioms can be accounted for more naturally and convincingly in another paradigm than in the Chomskyan paradigm. He classifies idioms in terms of their characteristics. First, he points out syntactically ill-formed idioms and well-formed ones. "Syntactically ill-formed" refers to unusual forms ordinary phrases do not have. Examples of ill-formed idioms include such expressions as *by and large, trip the light fantastic, kingdom come*, etc.

Some of these idioms are derived diachronically from non-idiomatic expressions or from cut-off versions of literary quotations. According to *Longman Dictionary of English Idioms* (1979), *kingdom come* comes from the Lord's Prayer in the Bible and *trip the light fantastic* from *L'Allegro* (1632) by John Milton:

> Come, and trip it as you go
> On the light fantastic toe.

By and large originally referred to keeping a ship on a course so that it is sailing at a good speed even though the direction of the wind is changing.

Second, he distinguishes idioms from semi-idioms whose idiomatic meanings remain even if they are passivized. *Bury the hatchet* is such an idiom, in which case, he thinks, idiomatic interpretation and the literal meaning are metaphorically related with each other.

Fraser (1970) notes that some idioms undergo some transformations but others do not, and that the behavior of idioms with regard to transformations has a certain regularity. He proposes a "Frozenness Hierarchy" of idioms in which idioms can be classified into seven levels of frozenness. The most significant feature of Fraser's claim is that any idiom marked as belonging to one level is automatically marked as belonging to any lower level. In other words, if an idiom belongs to a category such as L3, the idiom may undergo the operations of the lower categories L2 and L1. On the other hand, an idiom of L1 does not undergo any other applications except Adjunction operation. The hierarchy is suggested in (9) and the results of the application of transformations are in (10).

(9) L6 — Unrestricted: there is no example because this level presupposes transformational operations are inapplicable to idioms.
L5 — Reconstitution (the action nominalization): *lay down the law, let the cat out of the bag, pop the question, spill the*

beans, etc.

L4 — Extraction (the passive and prepositional phrase preposing): *break the ice, lose sight of, make up one's mind, make use of, pay attention to, think of, wait on, worry about*, etc.

L3 — Permutation (particle movement): *keep up one's guard, let one's hair down, put on a good face, put on some weight*, etc.

L2 — Insertion (adverbial placement): *depend on, give the back of, harp on, lend a hand to, look for, pay homage to, run into, stick to*, etc.

L1 — Adjunction (the gerundive nominalization): *blow off some steam, burn the candle at both ends, care for, insist on, kick the bucket, shoot the bull, stand for*, etc.

L∅ — Completely Frozen: the idioms of this class do not permit any transformational operations. *Build castles in the air, by accident, by and large, face the music, let off some steam, sit on pins and needles, trip the light fantastic, turn a deaf ear to*, etc.

(10) a. *blow off some steam* (L1)

　　① *He blew some steam off after he got home. (particle movement)

　　② *Some steam was blown off at the party. (the passive)

　　③ *Your blowing off of some steam surprised us. (the action nominalization)

　　b. *put on some weight* (L3)

　　① John has put some weight on.

② *Some weight has been put on by John.

③ *The putting on of some weight by Henry caused great alarm.

c. *make up one's mind* (L4)

① No one can make your mind up for you.

② Your mind can be made up by no one but you.

③ *Your making up of your own mind on that issue surprised us.

d. *lay down the law* (L5)

① Her father laid the law down when she came in at 4 a.m.

② The law was laid down by her father before she was even twelve.

③ His laying down of the law didn't impress anyone.

Cutler (1982) supports the above hierarchy by proposing that frozenness and age are related in some degree. She checks the earliest citation for the representative examples of Fraser's hierarchy against the Oxford English Dictionary. She shows that the more frozen an idiom is, the longer it has existed in the language.

Gibbs (1987) considers not only syntactic properties but also semantic properties. He proposes two criteria for dividing idiom types which are related with each other. The first one is related to whether idioms are syntactically frozen or syntactically flexible while the other is related to whether they are metaphorically transparent or opaque. In metaphorically transparent idioms, literal and figurative meanings are closely related; on the other hand they are not closely related in metaphorically opaque idioms. Of course, syntactic frozenness or flexibility and metaphorical transparency or opacity are the matter of degree. In other words, idioms constitute a continuum in syntactic behavior or in semantic interpretation. Syntactic behavior is associated with the way each individual word in an idiom contributes to the figurative interpretation, but syntactically frozen idioms are not always metaphorically opaque. Syntactically flexible idioms can also be metaphorically transparent or opaque idioms. In Gibbs's experiment *beat around the bush* is a syntactically flexible and metaphorically opaque idiom; its literal meaning is not closely related to its figurative meaning. *Sit on pins and needles* is a syntactically frozen and metaphorically transparent idiom. People easily guess its figurative meaning.

Therefore, idiomatic phrases differ in various linguistic and pragmatic dimensions. They do not form a homogeneous class in people's learning, understanding and remembering as well as in their syntactic behaviors and semantic interpretations.

Let us consider the idiom types suggested by Fillmore et al. (1988). First, he distinguishes encoding idioms from decoding idioms. In the case of encoding idioms, language users might or might not understand them without prior experience. Idioms like *answer the door* and *wide awake* are only encoding idioms. Decoding idioms cannot be interpreted with confidence if they are not learned separately. The expressions, *kick the bucket* and *pull a fast one*, are examples of both decoding and encoding idioms. The second distinction is made between grammatical and extragrammatical idioms. Grammatical idioms have words in a grammatical structure while extragrammatical idioms have words in an anomalous structure. Examples for the latter are *first off, sight unseen, all of a sudden, by and large*, etc. Thirdly, he proposes substantive and formal idioms. Substantive idioms are lexically filled idioms, whereas formal idioms are lexically open idioms. The latter idioms are syntactic patterns dedicated to semantic and pragmatic purposes which are not inferrable from their forms alone. *The X-er, the Y-er* construction belongs to the formal idioms. Fourth division is made between idioms with pragmatic point and idioms without pragmatic point. Idioms with special pragmatic purposes are *how do you do?, once upon a time*, etc. Idioms with contextually neutral purposes are *all of a sudden, by and large, the X −er the Y −er* and the like.

Gibbs and Nayak (1989) think that idioms constitute a continuum in analyzability, and that idioms differ in their degree of semantic decomposition. They divide idioms into semantically decomposable idioms, abnormally decomposable idioms and semantically non-decomposable idioms. In the case of normally decomposable idioms, the individual components share the same paradigmatic or syntagmatic semantic field with their idiomatic referents. The individual parts of semantically non-decomposable idioms like *kick the bucket* are not in the same semantic field as their respective figurative referents "to die" and their relation was once historical but now arbitrary to most speakers. So, non-decomposable idioms are lexicalized like long words and processed as such.

They show that syntactic productivity of idioms depends on their semantic composition. That is, the more analyzable an idiom is, the more syntactically productive it is. Abnormally decomposable idioms have metaphorical relation between the components and the referents. For example, we understand the idiom *let off steam* to mean "release tension from anger" because our knowledge maps a pressurized container with steam onto a person who is releasing tension from anger.

Glucksberg (1993) suggests three types following Cacciari and Glucksberg (1991): compositional−opaque idioms, compositional−transparent idioms, and quasi−metaphorical idioms. *Kick the bucket* is an example of compositional−opaque idioms, in which the constituents of the idiom have obscure relation with its meaning. But the meaning of each word may constrain the interpretation and use of the idiom. In the example, *kick the bucket*, people may not guess the meaning "to die" but they may agree to the fact that the act of kicking makes the action abrupt. That is to say, *kick the bucket* may not be used in the sense of slow dying.

In the case of compositional−transparent idioms, there exists one-to-one semantic relation between the components of the idiom and their meaning. *Break the ice* and *spill the beans* are such examples. *Break* means 'change a mood or feeling,' and *ice*, 'social tension' in break the ice. In *spill the beans, spill* refers to 'the act of revealing,' and *beans*, 'concealed or unknown material or information.' Compositional−transparent idioms include both Gibbs & Nayak's normally decomposable idioms and abnormally decomposable idioms.

Quasi−metaphorical idioms convey meaning via their allusional contents. They call to mind a prototypical or stereotypical instance of an entire category of people, events, situations, or actions (cf. Glucksberg 1993: 18). *Give up the ship, carry coals to Newcastle*, and *bury the hatchet* are such examples. The act of giving up the ship is an exemplar of surrendering and the action of burying the hatchet was a real part of making peace ritual.

In Chapter 4, I will have an experiment on English idioms according to the idiom types discussed in this section. To speak more concretely, I will explore to what extent the idiom types make an influence on the comprehension of idioms.

This study is concerned with idioms including metaphors and metonymies. Of course, all idioms do not contain metaphors and metonymies, but in many cases idioms are motivated by conceptual metaphors and they include metaphors and metonymies. In the next chapter, I study such underlying metaphors and metonymies represented in some idioms.

2. Metaphor and Metonymy

Metaphor and metonymy have been considered as stylistic devices in language and literature. But Lakoff and Johnson (1980) propose that they are problems not only of a language but also of the human conceptual system, and that a huge number of thinking processes are structured and defined metaphorically. Sweetser (1990) shows that even ordinary words we use in everyday lives contain conceptual metaphors and that we can see it from their etymologies. Metaphor and metonymy can be found anywhere in our everyday lives. In particular, most titles of magazines contain metaphors or metonymies. Such metaphors and metonymies are associated with culture and time, so that many foreigners or even native speakers who do not know about the current events or situations have difficulty in finding their meanings or implications.

According to Fromkin and Rodman (1993: 148 − 152), anomaly, metaphor and idioms have been considered as examples of rule violation. Anomaly is nonsense, whereas metaphor and idioms, at first glance, appear to be nonsensical but they convey particular ideas. Metaphorical use of language reflects linguistic creativity at its highest. Such an extended use of metaphor may sometimes be based on semantic properties that are inferred by some kind of similarity. But the basis of metaphorical use is the ordinary linguistic knowledge about words, their semantic properties, and their combining powers that all speakers possess. Let us consider some different views on metaphor.

1) Views on Metaphor

Early transformational grammarians regard metaphorical sentences as deviant because they break selectional restrictions.[2] But they think the deviant sentences can be interpreted by a direct analogy to well-formed sentences that observe the selectional rules. That is to say, metaphor was regarded as an inessential and deviant phenomenon of language. Chomsky (1965: 149) suggested examples like the following:

---

2) Selectional restrictions are rules which systematically select the verb in terms of the choice of subject and object (Chomsky 1965: 92).

(11) a. John plays golf.

     b. Golf plays John.

Chomsky's explanation is that (11a) is a well-formed sentence, and (11b) breaks selectional rules but can be interpreted metaphorically if an appropriate context is supplied. In other words, such sentence as (11b) can be interpreted by a direct analogy to the corresponding well-formed sentence like (11a) that observes the selectional rules.

In pragmatics metaphor is interpreted in terms of conversational implicature or conventional implicature. Grice (1975) regards metaphor as a deviance of conversational principle. According to him, metaphor flouts the maxim of quality; i.e., "try to make your contribution one that is true." He divides meaning into two categories: one is what is said, and the other is what is implicated. The former is made up of semantic meaning of a sentence, and the latter consists of conversational implicature and conventional implicature.

Searle (1979: 93) distinguishes speaker's utterance meaning from sentence meaning. The former is what a speaker means by uttering words, sentences and expressions, and the latter is what the words, sentences and expressions mean. Metaphorical meaning is always speaker's utterance meaning. The relation between the sentence meaning and the metaphorical speaker's meaning is systematic rather than random or ad hoc. According to such a pragmatic approach to metaphor, metaphor has double interpretations, namely, literal interpretation and figurative interpretation. If literal interpretation is inappropriate, it is rejected and figurative interpretation is accepted.

Recent studies and experiments deny the two-level interpretation of metaphor. Metaphorical expressions are understood as fast as literal expressions under enough context, so that additional processes are not necessary. The experiment by Ortony et al. (1978) shows that if there is a short or no context, metaphorical expressions take more time to understand than literal expressions. But it also shows that metaphorical expressions are understood as easily as literal expressions under enough context.

Schraw (1995) has similar experimental results. Context has an influence on the time to understand metaphors because metaphors, presented in limited context, may require additional processing effort. It takes time and effort to activate existing lexical and schematic knowledge necessary to comprehend metaphorical referents. Another result is that subjects or objects represented in an metaphorical expression are often recognized better than other words, which means that metaphorical expressions usually leave stronger impressions than comparable literal expressions. In other words, words are more recognizable when used metaphorically.

Hubbell and O'Boyle (1995) also explore the relation between metaphor and context. Extended context seems to play a prominently facilitative role in metaphorical interpretation. That is to say, extended context plays the same role as schema or semantic domain. A sentence such as *The old rock became brittle with age* (Hubbell and O'Boyle 1995: 272) may be interpreted literally in a geological sense but can also be interpreted metaphorically if it occurs in a discourse concerning a professor emeritus. Hence, the surrounding context provides support for the metaphorical interpretation.

Lakoff and Johnson (1980) propose that metaphorical concepts are systematic and they are grounded in our experiences. So, metaphor is not only a matter of language but also a matter of thought processes. It is pervasive in everyday life; thus, most of our conceptual systems are metaphorical in nature. That is to say, language is a part of general human cognition, and so is metaphor. Therefore, metaphor is understood through the same cognitive processes as we understand literal language.

2) Domains of Metaphor

Lakoff (1993: 5) suggests that metaphor involves understanding a domain of experience in terms of a very different domain of experience. That is, metaphor can be understood as a mapping from a "source domain" to a "target domain." For instance, in the metaphor LOVE IS A JOURNEY, we understand the domain of love (the target domain) in terms of the domain of journeys (the source domain) through the cross−domain mapping. "Target" means a described concept, and "source" is a comparison concept. In general, the target domain includes abstract things or concepts, while the source domain contains concrete things. Table 2 illustrates some examples of the source and target domains, which are from Lakoff and Johnson (1980) and Lakoff (1993).

Table 2. The Target Domain and The Source Domain

TARGET domain	SOURCE domain
anger	heat, steam, a dangerous animal
argument	war
communication	sending
theory	building
time	money, moving objects
understanding	seeing
love	war, journey
life	gambling game, journey
idea	food

McCabe (1983) studies a relationship of "tenor−vehicle"[3] similarity to the quality of metaphors. He develops the ideas of Brown (1958), who puts an emphasis on associatedness rather than shared physical resemblance in metaphoric quality. If tenor and vehicle are too similar, metaphor is too transparent, so that it is uninteresting, while if metaphor is too opaque, it is uninterpretable. Therefore, a moderate degree of similarity makes a good metaphor. But some linguists like Brooks (1965: 317) claim that the greater the disparity between the two domains is, i.e., the lesser the similarity is, the better the metaphor becomes. In fact, metaphoric comparisons of dissimilar objects are common in good writing. For instance, in Donne's "A Valediction: Forbidding Mourning," he compares the souls of two lovers to a drafting compass's legs. Similarly, Malgady and Johnson (1976) suggest "soft hair like shiny silk" is better metaphor than "long hair like elegant silk," because "soft" and "shiny" are related to

---

3) Tenor corresponds to the target domain, and vehicle to the source domain.

40

both "hair" and "silk" whereas "long" is only related to "hair," and "elegant" is only related to "silk."[4]

Some linguists suggest that there is another domain in addition to the source and the target domain. Fong (1988) proposes there exists a hybrid domain between the source and the target domain. For instance, let us consider a conventional metaphor, ARGUMENT IS WAR. We think argument is interpreted in terms of war. Her claim is that the argument domain is in tight correspondence with the war domain, and there is a hybrid domain ARGUMENT#WAR, whose existence is based on the following. First, the "argument" structure is different from the "war" structure. In war there are conflicts among warring states, rulers, army commanders and armies, and the physical conflict exists in the case of armies. In argument there is a conflict only between participants, and the conflict is not physical but abstract and metaphorical. That is to say, metaphorical army is inanimate or at least it is made up of non-volitional objects, so there is no central aspect of war in argument. Second, unlike the idea that the source domain organizes a specific view of the target domain, two major features of the target domain (here, argument) determine which aspects of the source domain (here, war) can be used in the metaphor. One feature is that the metaphor is dominated by the awareness that argument exists between two persons. The other feature is that the metaphor is highly constrained by abstract and non-physical nature of argument. In other words, the property of the target domain constrains the metaphor. The target domain interacts

---

4) Malgady & Johnson's (1976) example is indirectly quoted from McCabe (1983: 42).

with the source domain to make the hybrid domain, which is automatically invoked, and expressions are interpreted with respect to the hybrid domain.

Turner and Fauconnier (1998) suggest that there is a dynamic integration process for making a new blended mental space. One of their examples is "If Clinton were the Titanic, the iceberg would sink," in which the source domain includes the Titanic and the iceberg, while the target domain includes Clinton and the scandal. There is a partial cross−space mapping between two mental spaces, the source and the target domain. Clinton is the counterpart of the Titanic and the scandal is the counterpart of the iceberg. There is a blended space in which Clinton is the Titanic and the scandal is the iceberg. The blend has a causal and event shape structure that does not come from the source domain, the Titanic. In some cases, the central infer-ence of the metaphor cannot be projected from the source. If inference is projected from the source, Clinton should lose the presidency. On the contrary, Clinton survives the scandal. Therefore, there exists a blend space which has a causal structure and an event shape structure. In the blend the Titanic is unsinkable as a force, and it is possible for the iceberg to sink. The scandal−iceberg is the greatest conceivable threat, but the Clinton−Titanic survives even the greatest conceivable threat. Clinton's extreme superiority as a force and the extreme status of the scandal as a threat are made in the blend, where a predictive inference "Clinton will survive" is possible. This inference is neither available from the source nor from the target, but it is constructed in the blend and projected to the target to reframe it and give it new and clearer inferences.

They also mention the analysis on the emotions studied by Lakoff (1987). For instance, in the case of "anger," the correspondences like those in Table 3 are generally agreed through metaphor and metonymy. But they propose that the contents of the physiological reaction are gained not only from the target domain but also from the source domain. So, the correspondences like those in Table 4 are suggested.

Table 3. The Source and the Target Domain of ANGER

SOURCE	TARGET	
"physical events"	"emotions"	"physiology"
container	person	person
heat	anger	body heat
steam	sign of anger	perspiration, redness
explode	show extreme anger	acute shaking, loss of physiological control
boiling point	highest degree of emotion	

Blend is associated with Input spaces and inferences made in the blend are projected to the Target Input Spaces. The structure of blend highly depends on the conventional metaphorical mapping from heat to anger. Yet blend provides a frame not available in the source nor in the target. To sum up, in contrast to the unidirectional mapping from the source onto the target domain, the theory with the blend space creates meaning through blending from the input spaces—source and target.

Table 4. The Blend with the Source and the Target Domain of ANGER

SOURCE	BLEND	TARGET	
Input Space 1	Blended Space	Input Space 2	Input Space 3
"physical events"		"emotions"	"physiology"
container	person / container	person	person
heat	heat / anger	anger	body heat
steam	steam / smoke	sign of anger	perspiration, redness
explode	explode	show extreme anger	acute shaking, loss of physiological control
boiling point	boiling / highest degree of emotion	highest degree of emotion	

Now, four-space model is suggested by some linguists like Fauconnier and Turner (1998). The four spaces are two input spaces, a source space and a target space, and two middle spaces, a generic space and a blended space. The generic space has an abstract structure which is made up of the common conceptual factors. The blended space inherits some conceptual factors from the two input spaces and it creates a new emergent structure. Let's take an example, *This surgeon is a butcher*.[5] According to the four-space model supporters, the mapping from the source domain to the target domain cannot explain the metaphor, the surgeon's incapability. In the Blended Theory of the four-space model, the meaning of the surgeon's incapability is taken from the following reasoning processes. First, the blended space inherits the conceptual factor 'a professional status healing human diseases' from the input space 1 of the source domain,

---

5) The example and the figure are indirectly quoted from Lee (2000).

and it inherits the conceptual factor 'a humble status butchering cows or pigs' from the input space 2 of the target domain. Second, the generic space has representations of the conceptual factors from the two input spaces. In other words, 'surgeon' and 'butcher' are represented into 'agents', 'operating room' and 'butcherin place' into 'working place', 'patients' and 'cows or pigs' into 'objects', 'a surgical knife' and 'butchering knife' into 'means', and 'a medical treatment' and 'meat supply' into 'purpose'. In the blended space, a new emergent structure is created by way of the mappings between the inherited conceptual structures and the factors of two input spaces. In the emergent structure, the purpose of the surgeon's operation is not consistent with the means of the butcher's butchery. The inference 'incapability' comes from this inconsistency. The conceptual integration is figured like the following.

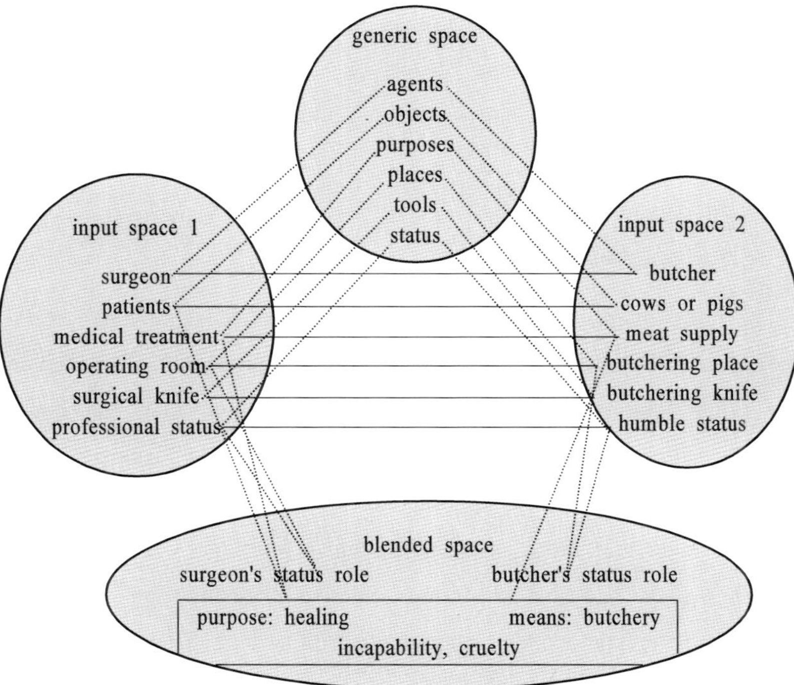

Figure 1. The Conceptual Integration Aspects in Blended Theory

3) Properties of Metaphor and Metonymy

Metaphor and metonymy are different processes. Metaphor, in a broad sense, includes metonymy, synecdoche, and hyperboles, while, in a narrow definition, it contrasts with metonymy. The former is that people understand and experience one kind of thing in terms of another, and the latter means that one entity stands for another in the same conceptual domain. The main function of metonymy is referring, while that of metaphor is understanding. Both metaphoric and metonymic concepts are systematic and they give structures to our thoughts, attitudes and behaviors, and they are based on our experience.

(1) Properties of Metaphor

The more intensive attitude of communicators tends to make metaphors easy because of the communicative property of metaphor. Generally, figurative languages are more pervasive than the corresponding literal languages, partly because figurative languages are more impressive and more unforgettable. Renee and Clevenger (1990) propose that the more knowledge on a certain concept makes metaphor easy, and that the more affective evaluation on a concept makes more metaphors than neutral evaluation does. They make these claims and they support through experiments that their claims are right. This shows that human thoughts and emotions are related and that especially intensive emotions are more motivating in making metaphors.

Let us consider the properties of metaphor.[6] The first property is conventionality. In general, it is related to the novelty of metaphor. The more novel a metaphorical expression is, the less conventional it is. Some linguists regard a conventionalized metaphor as a dead metaphor, and they think that the dead metaphor has no more metaphoricity, so that it cannot get a new literal meaning. Cognitive

---

6) The following discussion about the properties of metaphor is mainly based on Saeed (1997: 305).

linguists, however, suggest that the familiar conventionalized metaphors may get a new life and keep the metaphorical status. For example, the UP−DOWN metaphor is familiar and conventionalized, but it is continuously extended in our lives, e.g., to the names of drugs, *uppers* and *downers*. Lakoff (1993: 9) also argues for novel extensions of conventional metaphors. In his example, the song lyric, *we're driving in the fast lane on the freeway of love*, we understand exciting but dangerous love relationship. Such a comprehension is possible because the LOVE IS A JOURNEY metaphor is already part of our conceptual system. Like idioms, metaphor also constitutes a continuum scale from the conventional to the highly unconventional and unintelligible. Metaphor can be made at any place of the continuum scale. Conventional metaphors locate near the conventional end, while novel metaphors near the unconventional and unintelligible end. Generally the interpretation of metaphor depends on the context. Conventional metaphors can be understood by most competent speakers. But novel metaphors may be used at an atypical context, so that they need to be reevaluated in terms of the new context.

Second, metaphorical expressions have systematicity in the mapping between the source and the target domains. In the case of the metaphor, LOVE IS A JOURNEY, the following correspondences characterize the mapping (cf. Lakoff 1993: 6):

i) The lovers correspond to travelers.

ii) The love relationship corresponds to the vehicle.

iii) The lovers' common goals correspond to their common destinations on the journey.

iv) Difficulties in the relationship correspond to impediments to travel.

Third, metaphorical mapping is asymmetrical. In other words, it is unidirectional because mapping is made in one direction. Life is described in terms of journeys, but a journey is not described in terms of life. This directionality is something to do with the degree of abstractness, because, in most cases, metaphor is used to represent the abstract in terms of the concrete.[7] The common and everyday experiences of journey are used to characterize the processes of birth, death, ageing, etc.

(2) Properties of Metonymy

Metonymic concepts, as well as metaphoric concepts, give a structure to human language, thoughts, and behaviors, and they are based on human experiences. Metonymy brings meaning changes by contiguity of space, time, or cause and effect among meanings. In other words, in metonymy, a subcategory or a member of a category is used to stand for the category. Therefore, metonymy is not a cross −domain mapping but a mapping within a domain or a model.[8]

---

7) Of course, both source and target can be concrete. But in many cases, concrete lexical items may be used to represent more abstract concepts, which is called metaphorical extension. In the Grammaticalization Theory, metaphors have more inclusive concepts including the phenomenon that concrete lexical referents are used as abstract grammatical markers by metaphorical extension.

8) In the Grammaticalization Theory, Traugott and König (1991: 210) mention three types of contiguity in metonymy. The first type is contiguity in socio-physical or socio-cultural experience. For instance, the Latin word *coxa* 'hip' became French *cuisse* 'thigh', which indicates that the parts of the body are spatially contiguous in the physical world. The meaning of *boor* 'farmer' was developed into 'crude person,' which is an association of behavior with a certain person or class of people. The second type is

Lakoff (1987: 84) suggests the following characteristics of the meto-nymic idealized cognitive model.

i) There is a target concept A to be understood for some purpose in some context.

ii) There is a conceptual structure containing both A and another concept B.

iii) B is either part of A or closely associated with it in that conceptual structure. Typically, a choice of B will uniquely determine A, within that conceptual structure.

iv) Compared to A, B is either easier to understand, easier to remember, easier to recognize, or more immediately useful for the given purpose in the given context.

v) A metonymic model is a model of how A and B are related in a conceptual structure; the relationship is specified by a function from B to A.

Lakoff and Johnson (1980) show that there are many types of metonymic models for categories. First, the name of a container refers to the contents of the container. In *The kettle is boiling, the kettle* means the water within the kettle. Second, producer's names refer to the products. In the example, *Do you own any Picasso's?*, *Picasso's* represents works by Picasso. Third, a salient part makes reference to the whole. In *We need some new faces around here,*

---

contiguity in the utterance, often ending in ellipsis. One of the examples is the case of French *ne...pas*, which became *pas*. The third type is synecdoche or the part−whole relation. For instance, *redbreast* refers to 'robin' and *fingernail* represents *finger*, and *finger* refers to *hand*. In both cases, a part represents a whole.

faces mean persons. Fourth, the name of institutions stands for an individual or a group of individuals. For instance, in *The Government has stated..., the Government* refers to a person or a group of persons in the Government. Fifth, the names of places stand for the institutions in the places and important persons related to the institutions. The example is *negotiations between Washington and Moskow* where *Washington* and *Moskow* refer to the American government and the Russian government, respectively. Sixth, a token may refer to the type. In *This jacket is our best-selling item, this jacket* does not mean that the particular jacket had sold many times, but that jackets made to that design have sold well.

People use metonymic device in their everyday lives, but they do not notice it. Let us take some Korean examples.[9]

> (12) a. *congali ket −e!*
>
> the calves of the leg tuck up − Imp
>
> (lit.) Tuck up the calves of the leg!
>
> (int.) Tuck up the clothes of the calves!
>
> b. Lee Young −Pyo han −pang −ey 'manlicangseng' −i walulu
>
> (The Chosun Ilbo, 29, July, 2000)
>
> Lee Young −Pyo one shot −Inst 'the Great Wall of China'

---

9) The transliteration system used here for the Korean data is an extended version of the Yale Transliteration System. And the list of abbreviations are as follows:

Acc ⇒ Accusative; Comp ⇒ Complementizer; Dat ⇒ Dative; Fut ⇒ Future tense; Gen ⇒ Genitive; Imp ⇒ Imperative; Inst ⇒ Instrumental; Int. ⇒ Intended meaning; Inter ⇒ Interrogative; Lit. ⇒ Literal meaning; Loc ⇒ Locative; Nom ⇒ Nominative; Par ⇒ Particle; Past ⇒ Past tense; Top ⇒ Topic.

－Nom clattering down

(lit.) The Great Wall of China is clattering down by Lee Young－Pyo's one shot

(int.) The Chinese football team is clattering down by Lee Young－Pyo's one shot

Most people do not recognize that metonymy is involved in the above examples. In (12a), *congali* stands for the clothes covering the calves, and in (12b) everybody understands *'manlicanseng'* refers to China where it is located, and to speak more exactly, China stands for the Chinese football team. This is a kind of a part－whole metonymy. First, the part *manlicangseng* represents the whole, *China*, and second, the whole *China* stands for the part, *Chinese football team.*

4) Conceptual Metaphors

Gibbs and O'Brien (1990) raised a question: Why do several different idiomatic phrases represent similar meanings? They had some experiments, in which they investigated mental images on several different idiomatic expressions. The result is that several idioms, which have different surface forms, show high consistency in their images. The examples are *spill the beans, let the cat out of the bag,* and *blow the lid off.* The traditional view that the meanings of idioms are arbitrary cannot answer the following questions: i) Why are there many idioms referring to one concept?[10) ii) Why do the idioms have conventional images? iii) Why do the speakers have specific knowledge on the images? iv) Why is there high degree of similarity in speakers' answers on the questions about the specific knowledge on the images?

These phenomena are based on conceptual metaphors. Then, what are conceptual metaphors? They are supposed to underlie speakers' subconscious knowledge. For example, in the idiom *spill the beans, beans* refers to 'idea' or 'secret,' and *spill* means 'the act of revealing the secret.' Therefore, *spill the beans* does not mean 'to reveal a secret' accidentally, but we subconsciously understand the metaphorical mapping between the source domain and the target domain. That is to say, we understand mind as a container, and ideas as physical entities. The conceptual metaphors MIND IS A CONTAINER and IDEAS ARE PHYSICAL ENTITIES are in our conceptual system and shape the way we think and behave.

We do not notice such conceptual metaphors but in everyday lives we use the following expressions:

> (13) a. *ku −uy mal −un   na −uy maum −ul mengtulkey −*
> *hayssta*
> he − Gen words − Top I − Gen mind − Acc bruise − Past
> (lit.) His words bruised my mind.
> (int.) His words bruised my feelings.

---

10) According to the traditional view of idioms, there is no particular reason why each of these different phrases means "to reveal a secret." The link between an idiom and its figurative meaning is arbitrary and cannot be predicted from the meaning of its individual words. (Gibbs and O'Brien 1990: 36)

b. *ku —nun na —uy mitum —ul kkay peli —essta*

he—Top I—Gen belief—Acc break throw—Past away

(lit.) He broke and threw away my belief.

(int.) He frustrated my belief.

In (13a) and (13b), mind and belief, the words that indicate mental state, are used in the context of physical expression. That is to say, in Korean, also, the conceptual metaphors MIND IS A PHYSICAL OBJECT and BELIEF IS A PHYSICAL OBJECT are in our conceptual system.

Another conceptual metaphor we can easily find out in our everyday lives is LIFE IS WAR. In everyday lives we usually use such words as 'traffic war in the morning,' 'entrance examination war,' etc. Everything in our life does not match that of war, but parts of our life can be explained by the concept of war.

In order to see if any coherent conceptual structure emerged, Lakoff and Kövecses studied expressions of emotions in English. According to Lakoff (1987: 377), emotional concepts are very clear examples of concepts that are abstract and yet have an obvious basis in bodily experience. He shows that there are coherent conceptual organizations underlying many emotional expressions, among which several expressions are metaphorical and several ones are metonymical.

The most general conceptual metaphor that is involved in anger is ANGER IS HEAT. The physiological appearances referring to anger are body heat, internal pressure, agitation, and loss of control. Increased body heat motivates redness in the face or in the neck area, and such redness refers to anger metonymically. The example is *get hot under the collar.*

The most interesting fact is that the expressions referring to anger have upward orientation. Lakoff (1987) suggests that if the intensity of anger increases, fluid rises to the upper point. His examples are *Tears welled up, Anger kept building up,* etc. The intense heat makes steam, and intense anger produces pressure at the container, mind. The examples are *blow off steam, get steamed up,* and *let off steam.* Just as a part of a container goes up in the air, so a person's body-part goes up in the air when exploding. Such idioms are *blow one's stack, blow one's top, flip one's lid, hit the ceiling,* and *go through the roof.* Anger is mapped to heat or steam, so it may have full internal pressure until it arrives at the point of exploding. Therefore, all these ideas have upward orientation. When something explodes, the internal thing comes out, which can be elaborated up to animals' giving birth. *Have kittens* and *have a cow* are the examples.

Anger may lead to loss of control, which can be dangerous. Therefore, the conceptual metaphor ANGER IS INSANITY makes other conceptual metaphors through metaphor and metonymy. The metaphorical link between insanity and anger makes expressions referring to insane behavior represent angry behavior. Insane behavior means insanity, and insanity represents anger, and therefore insane behavior stands for anger. So, a metonymy INSANE BEHAVIOR STANDS FOR INSANITY comes out. The examples are *have a fit, foam at the mouth, fit to be tied,* and *throw a tantrum.* Violent behavior is also regarded as a form of insane behavior, so there is a metonymy like VIOLENT FRUSTRATED BEHAVIOR STANDS FOR ANGER over the idioms such as *tear one's hair out, bang one's head against the wall*, and *climb the walls*. The ANGER IS A DANGEROUS ANIMAL metaphor is also the basis of other conceptual metaphors of anger. The ANGRY BEHAVIOR IS AGGRESSIVE ANIMAL BEHAVIOR metaphor is one of those metaphors and includes such idioms as *get one's hackles up, bare one's teeth, ruffle one's feathers, bridle with anger, bite one's head off*, and *jump down one's throat*. Aggressive behavior corresponds to angry behavior metaphorically and it also refers to anger metonymically. Therefore, idioms like *look daggers at* contain a metonymy AGGRESSIVE VISUAL BEHAVIOR STANDS FOR ANGER. The following shows the metaphors and metonymies related with anger.

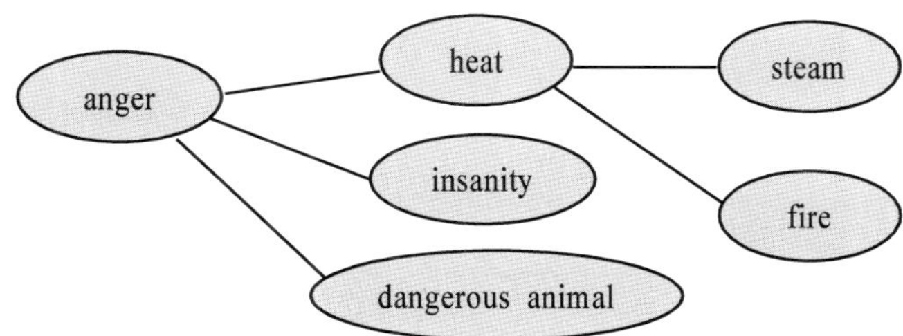

Figure 2. Metaphors of ANGER

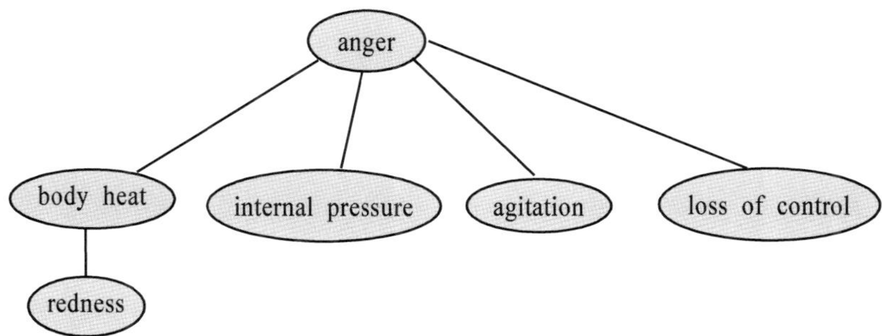

Figure 3. Metonymies of ANGER

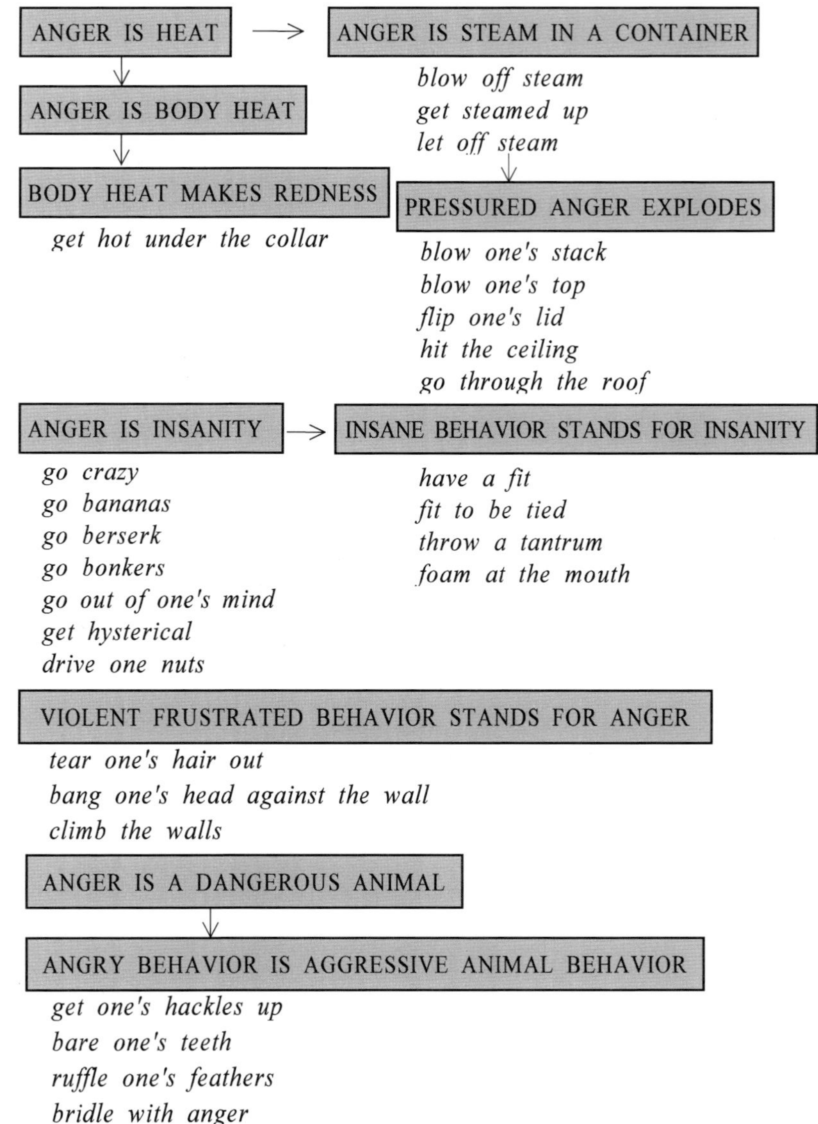

Figure 4. Conceptual metaphors and metonymies of ANGER

Figure 4 shows the conceptual metaphors and metonymies and idioms involved in anger.

Now, let us consider other emotions like love and joy. Generally, emotional effects are understood in terms of physical entities or physical contact. In other words, the conceptual metaphor EMOTION IS A PHYSICAL ENTITY shapes our language and thought. We usually say *That idea bowled me over, That really made an impression on me*, etc. And we take emotions like love as an entity with a boundary. The typical idiom is *fall in love.*

Lakoff (1993) provides strong evidence for conceptual metaphors. In the case of the metaphor LOVE IS A JOURNEY, there is a general principle governing how linguistic expressions about journey are used to characterize love, and how our patterns of inference about journeys are used to reason about love when the expressions about journey are used. It is a principle for understanding the domain of love in terms of the domain of journey, and it is a part of the conceptual system underlying English. The metaphor can be understood as a mapping from a source domain (in this case, journey) to a target domain (in this case, love), so that the entities in the domain of love correspond systematically to those in the domain of a journey.

The following are conceptual metaphors of love and their examples.

Table 5. Conceptual Metaphors of Love

positive metaphors	neutral metaphors	negative metaphors
LOVE IS A NUTRIENT LOVE IS APPETIZING FOOD LOVE IS MAGIC THE OBJECT OF LOVE IS A GOODNESS	LOVE IS A JOURNEY	LOVE IS WAR LOVE IS HUNTING LOVE IS A DISEASE LOVE IS MADNESS LOVE IS A PATIENT

LOVE IS MAGIC

She *cast her spell* over me.

He has me *in a trance*.

LOVE IS NUTRIENT

I was *given new strength* by her love.

I *thrive on* love.

I'm *starved for* your affection.

I'm *drunk with* love.

He is *sustained by* love.

LOVE IS A JOURNEY

Our relationship has hit *a dead-end street*.

Our relationship is *off the track*.

The marriage is *on the rocks*.

We are *spinning our wheels*.

LOVE IS A PATIENT

Their marriage is *on the mend*.

Their relationship is *in really good shape*.

Their marriage is *on its last legs*.

LOVE IS WAR

She *fought for* him, but his mistress *won out*.

She is *besieged by* suitors.

He *made an ally of* her mother.

LOVE IS MADNESS

She *drives me out of my mind.*

I'm *crazy about* her.

Joy is compared to priceless commodities or something to strive for, and to light or life. *Joy* has an UP image−schema, so the following idioms have the conceptual metaphor JOY IS UP: *cheer up, I'm six feet off the ground, I'm on cloud nine, she's walking on air. Joy* as well as *anger* takes the UP direction probably because it is natural that emotions are spouted out to the UP direction.

To sum up, the speakers' subconscious knowledge on conceptual metaphors may motivate the meaning of idioms, and such subconscious knowledge is revealed by investigating the mental images on some idioms. Namely, the speakers' mental images offer the linking between idioms and their figurative meanings. And the conceptual metaphors give coherence to several idioms which have similar figurative meanings. But the meanings of all idioms are not motivated by conceptual metaphors. There are idioms not motivated by conceptual metaphors such as *kick the bucket.* And there are idioms which do not have well-formed mental images like *make the scene.* Therefore, conceptual metaphors can constrain mental images of idioms, but it does not mean that they make the meanings of idioms predictable. They make the figurative meaning of idioms not arbitrary.

In general, conceptual metaphors are basic-level metaphors (Lakoff 1987: 407), which make us understand and infer certain concepts, using our knowledge on familiar and well-structured domains. For example, the target domains of anger contain abstract concepts—ENTITY,

INTENSITY, LIMIT, FORCE, and CONTROL, whereas the source domains include basic-level concepts—HOT FLUID, INSANITY, FIRE, BURDEN, and STRUGGLE. The basic-level concepts are directly linked to our experience, and they are information-rich and rich in conventional mental imagery. The HOT FLUID metaphor and the FIRE metaphor help us understand which type of entity anger is. The INSANITY and the STRUGGLE metaphor give us a sense of what is involved in controlling anger. Without such metaphors, our understanding of anger might be considerably impoverished. Table 6 shows the conceptual metaphors associated with several idiomatic expressions.

Table 6. The Conceptual Metaphors and Associated Idioms

CONCEPT	CONCEPTUAL METAPHORS	ASSOCIATED IDIOMS
ANGER	ANGER IS HEAT ANGER IS STEAM IN ACONTAINER MIND IS A CONTAINER ANGER IS ANIMAL BEHAVIOR ANGER IS INSANITY	blow one's stack hit the ceiling lose one's cool foam at the mouth flip one' lid get steamed up blow off the steam let off steam go crazy drive one nuts go bananas go berserk go out of one's mind go bonkers get hysterical
INSANITY	MIND IS A CONTAINER MIND IS A BRITTLE OBJECT INSANITY IS AN INVISIBLE FORCE SANITY IS AN ENTITY THAT CAN BE LOST	go off one's rocker lose one's marbles lose one's grip go to pieces bounce off the walls

CONCEPT	CONCEPTUAL METAPHORS	ASSOCIATED IDIOMS
CONTROL or AUTHORITY	CONTROL IS A POSSESSION CONTROL IS AN INVISIBLE FORCE	crack the whip call the shots keep the ball rolling lay down the law wear the pants
SECRETIVE-NESS or REVELATION	SECRET IS AN ENTITY IN A CONTAINER IDEAS ARE PHYSICAL ENTITIES	keep it under one's hat button one' lips hold one's tongue behind one's back keep in the dark spill the beans let the cat out of the bag blow the whistle blow the lid off loose lips
SIGHT	VISUAL FIELDS ARE CONTAINERS	lose sight of out of sight

CHAPTER 3

Cognitive Linguistic Explanations of Idioms

Most words have not only the basic and central meaning but also extended meanings. Among the ways of extending meanings, two most important processes are metaphor and metonymy. Generally, metonymy is considered as a more basic process than metaphor, because metonymy is based on contiguity whereas metaphor has a tendency to depend on convention or culture. Foreign students learning English may understand meanings extended through metonymies better than those through metaphors.

Now, let us consider some idioms with metaphors and metonymies. They show a certain degree of consistency in terms of the basic concepts and mental images which they make. Idioms with color terms and body-part terms will be discussed in this chapter.

1. Color Term Idioms

It appears that every language has metaphors and metonymies of color terms. Color makes people have some feelings. In other words, color is a part of our conceptual knowledge, so that we can recognize certain meanings conveyed by some colors. Not only color terms themselves but also their meanings may vary across cultures, so that some color terms have common meanings throughout cultures, while other color terms have different meanings culture after culture. Also, they have radial categories extended from the basic and central meaning.[11]

Berlin and Kay (1969) explored basic color terms and some special ordering among them. The latter is expressed in the form of an implicational hierarchy as illustrated in Figure 5, where the existence of a category to the right of an arrow implies the existence of all the categories to its left in a language:

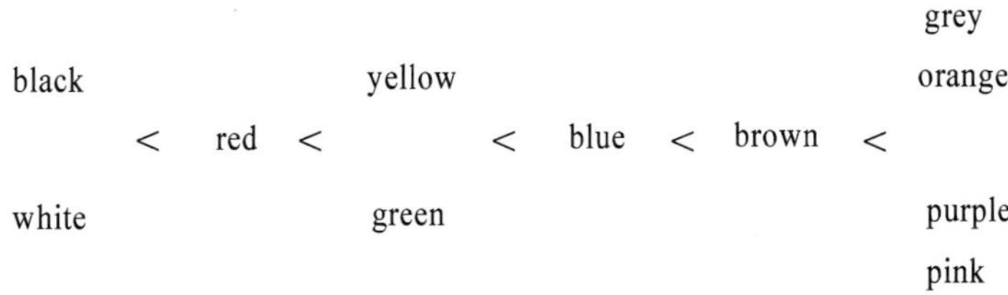

Figure 5. Implicational Hierarchy of Basic Color Terms

---

11) For radial category structure, see Lakoff (1987: 91−114).

The above hierarchy has been generally considered to correspond with the number of idioms the color terms make. In other words, *black, white* and *red* make more idioms than other colors, and *blue* makes more idioms than *purple* or *pink*. In case of English, however, the number of idioms color terms make does not always correspond with the hierarchy. Taylor (1989: 12) proposes that the position on the hierarchy tends to correlate with the productivity of derivational processes. On the whole, the terms at the very left of the hierarchy tend to undergo the derivational processes with the suffix *-en* or the suffix *-ness: whiten, blacken, redden*(cf. **bluen, *yellowen, *pinken*, etc); *whiteness, blueness, greyness*(cf. **purpleness, *orangeness*).

In this section six focal color terms are discussed. *Black* and *white* are treated together in section 3.1.1, and *red, green, yellow,* and *blue* are studied together in section 3.1.2.

1) Black and White

In this section, I will examine idiomatic expressions containing the color terms *black* and *white*, as illustrated in (1) through (6).

(1) *black* − Metonymy
(2) *white* − Metonymy
(3) − (4) *black* − Metaphor
(5) − (6) *white* − Metaphor

Let us consider the idioms in (1), which involve the color term *black*.

    (1) a. They beat him *black and blue*.

        b. They *worked like a black* every day.

        c. Our account *is in the black* this month.

The above expressions are based on metonymy. *Black and blue* of (1a) refers to the skin darkly discolored as the result of being beaten. Such a metonymic use can also be found in the sentence, *If he says that again, I'll give him a black eye. A black eye* means an eye which is made black by a blow.

Black of (1b) means a slave, because black people worked as slaves in America and their skin color is black. The skin color, which is a part of a body, refers to the person with the body. We can say that this is THE SKIN COLOR FOR THE PERSON metonymy.

Be in the black in (1c) means having money in a bank account or showing a profit, which is the opposite of the expression *be in the red*. This is also used in Korean in the form of Chinese characters like *hukca* 'in the black letters' or *cekca* 'in the red letters (of an account book).' This is also a kind of THE PART FOR THE WHOLE metonymy because the color of letters represents the letters.

    (2) a. *white collar workers, white collar jobs*

        b. He looked *as white as a sheet*.

        c. She *turned white* with terror.

        d. They walked towards the enemy waving *the white flag*.

White of (2a) refers to the color of clothes. *White collar workers* represent office workers or indoor workers who do not do physical or dirty work with their hands.

As white as a sheet of (2b) represents paleness in the face because of illness or great fear.[12] Because turning white may be due to fear or terror, *white* stands for the emotion of fear as in (2c). Such phrases as *white lips* or *white-faced* also mean the paleness with fear. From fear or terror *white* may also convey negative connotations like surrender as in *a white flag* of (2d). Similarly, the expression *white feather* is a sign of unwillingness to fight because of lack of courage.

Next, let us consider idioms with some conceptual metaphors.

> (3) Suddenly everything *went black* and that's the last thing I
>   can remember.

Go black in (3) is represented to disappear from sight because someone has fainted or become unconscious. So, *black* in (3) means both physical and mental darkness. Here, the expression is based on the conceptual metaphor, PSYCHOLOGICAL EVENT IS A PHYSICAL EVENT.

The following expressions are based on the conceptual metaphor QUALITY IS A COLOR.

---

12) Korean also has the same expression.
    (elkwul −i) paikcicang kath −ta
    face−Nom white−paper−sheet be like
    (lit.) (His) face is like white−paper−sheet
    (int.) (His face) looks as white as a sheet

68

(4) a. The bad news we've been getting means that things *look
very black* for us.

b. You always *look on the black side*.

c. We are *in his black books* because we didn't invite him
to our party.

d. They bought butter on the *black market*.

e. The name *Tatkenski* is on the *black list* of the Secret
Police.

f. I'm the *black sheep* of the family because my brother is
a lawyer and my sister is a doctor but I decided to be
an actor.

Look on the black side in (4b) is opposite to *look on the bright
side*, so *black* can be changed into *dark*. *Black* means not only
darkness but also badness. From (4a) to (4c), *black* refers to
badness; in (4d) it means unlawfulness; in (4e) it represents
untrustworthiness; and in (4f) it conveys worthlessness. *In someone's
black books* of (4c) means disfavor with someone. Instead of *black,
bad* can be used without the change of meaning. *A black market* is
a market where unlawful buying and selling of goods are made. *A
black list* means a list of people or organizations that have caused
offence or are regarded as untrustworthy, disloyal, etc. *A black sheep*
is a worthless member of a respectable group. These expressions can
be understood by way of the conceptual metaphors, BADNESS IS
BLACK, UNLAWFULNESS IS BLACK, UNTRUSTWORTHINESS
IS BLACK, and DISLOYALTY IS BLACK which are the sub-stage
conceptual metaphors of QUALITY IS A COLOR. With regard to

those conceptual metaphors, there are a series of reasoning processes: 'Black is dark'; 'In darkness nothing can be seen'; 'Seeing is understanding'; 'What we understand is what we can believe'; and 'What we cannot believe is not good'. The conceptual metaphor BADNESS IS BLACK is also found in the examples like *black magic* which is done with the help of the devil, *black art* which is a magic used for evil purposes, *black humor* or *black comedy* which means humor or comedy dealing with unpleasant or dangerous people or states of affairs.

The color term *white* is involved in the contrastive conceptual metaphors.

> (5) a. I told his mother *a white lie* and said that he was well and back at work.
> b. *white magic*
> c. *white witch*
> d. *Two blacks don't make a white.*
> e. *make one's name white again*

White lie in (5a) is a lie with good intentions in order to save someone's feeling from being hurt. *White magic* of (5b) is a magic used for good purpose, and *white witch* of (5c) is a good witch. The meaning of (5d) is that two wrongs don't make a right. These expressions contain such conceptual metaphor as GOODNESS IS WHITE. The color term *white* in (5e) represents innocence, where the conceptual metaphor, INNOCENCE IS WHITE, is contained. The white color reminds people of a spotless clean image. Actually the word *whiteness* means innocence.

(6) The housing associations are one of *the white hopes* of the housing movement.

The (great) white hope of (6) means a person who is expected to bring fame, glory, victory to a team of which he / she is a representative. According to *Longman Dictionary of English Idioms* (1979), the phrase was originally used to refer to a white fighter in boxing who was attempting to beat a black fighter. Black boxers often held the first place in the sport. The phrase *white man* means not only a white-skinned man but also a good man. It may be the product of racial discrimination. So, metonymy which refers to body color and the conceptual metaphor GOODNESS IS WHITE make the expression.

These conceptual metaphors, BADNESS IS BLACK, UNLAWFUL-NESS IS BLACK, GOODNESS IS WHITE and INNOCENCE IS WHITE, are found in Korean, too. The following expressions are from Korean.

(7) *huk —paik —ul kali —ta*
black — white — Acc distinguish
(lit.) to distinguish black from white
(int.) to distinguish bad from good

(8) a. *hukmak*
(lit.) a black curtain
(int.) concealed circumstances

   b. *sok −i kem −ta*

      inside −Nom be.black

      (lit.) The inside is black.

      (int.) (Someone) is evil-hearted.

   c. *kem −un son*

      black hand

      (lit.) a black hand

      (int.) an evil hand

And there is a title of a children's story in Korean, *hayan nekwuli, kkaman mapepsa* 'White Raccoon, Black Witch.' The title makes people guess the story. The raccoon is good and the witch is bad.

2) Red, Green, Yellow and Blue

Major conceptual metaphors related to *red* and *blue* are EMOTION IS A COLOR and TEMPERATURE IS A COLOR. EMOTION IS A COLOR has sub-stage conceptual metaphors: ANGER IS RED, ENVY IS GREEN, and MELANCHOLY IS BLUE. *Red* is associated with emotions such as anger, embarrassment, or excitement, because we take red color on our face in such emotions. Lakoff (1987: 382) explains that increased body heat and / or blood pressure is assumed to cause redness in the face and neck area, and such redness can also metonymically indicate anger.

(9) a. He is no friend of mine—it makes me *see red* every
time I hear his name.

b. Any letter of complaint to the boss is *like a red rag to
the bull.*

c. I *was my face red* when I suddenly discovered that I
had forgotten to bring any money out with me and
couldn't pay for my bus ride.

d. They heard this morning that they've passed their exam-
inations, so they've gone out *to paint the town red.*

The phrase *see red* in (9a) means 'to become violently angry.'
Like a red rag to the bull in (9b) refers to the large piece of red
cloth waved by bullfighters in Spain to make the bull attack. Here
also, *red* is used to cause great annoyance or anger. *Red* of *be
someone's face red* in (9c) means confusion, surprise, or embarrassment. *To paint the town red* in (9d) is represented to have a very
enjoyable time in a lively and noisy manner, so *red* means excitement.
The color terms, *green* and *blue* represent the emotions like envy
and melancholy, respectively.

(10) a. She'll be *green with envy* when I tell her that I've
bought myself a new car.

b. I'm *feeling* rather *blue* today.

Green is the color representing envy as in (10a). *A green eye* also
means eyes with envy. In (10b) the color *blue* stands for melancholy.
The color term *blue* in *blue Monday, be in the blue, have the blue,*

and *look blue*, is also metaphorically understood as melancholy. The conceptual metaphors ENVY IS GREEN and MELANCHOLY IS BLUE provide grounds for those metaphorical expressions.

The conceptual metaphor TEMPERATURE IS A COLOR permeates our everyday lives. When it is hot or warm, the color *red* occurs to us. When it is cold, we relate it with the color *blue*. In other words, HOTNESS IS RED and COLDNESS IS BLUE are the sub-stage conceptual metaphors of TEMPERATURE IS A COLOR. In the Korean stock market, the red figures refer to going up of the stock index and the blue figures indicate falling down. The following expressions are understood in the same context.

(11) a. *thwuca shimli −ey pwul −ul pwuthi −ta*
      investment mind−Loc fire−Acc make
      (lit.) to make a fire to the investment mind
      (int.) to make a fire to the mind for investment
   b. *thwuca shimli −ka kukto −lo ele −pwut −ess −ta*
      investment mind−Nom extremely freeze−Past
      (lit.) Investment mind was extremely frozen.
      (int.) Mind for investment was extremely frozen.

(11a) reminds us of heat or red color and (11b) is associated with coldness or blue color. But let us consider the following expressions.

(12) a. Our account *is in the black* this month.
   b. Our account *is in the red*.

When one takes out more money from a bank than one has in one's account, this is sometimes indicated by figures printed in red on one's bank statement. Therefore, *in the red* in (12b) means being in debt, and this is the opposite of *in the black.* The expressions such as *go into the red* and *go out of the red* are similar examples. In the American stock market, the red color of figures indicates falling down, whereas the black color of figures represents going up.

In Korea, red letters are used somewhat incoherently. The words in sino-Korean word *cekca* 'in the red letters' and *hukca* 'in the black letters' correspond to the American usage, while in the Korean stock market, the red figures refer to going up and the blue figures indicate falling down. Such incoherence may be explained by different kinds of experiential basis suggested in Lakoff and Johnson (1980: 19 − 20).

The role of the experiential basis is important in understanding the workings of metaphors that do not fit together because they are based on different kinds of experience. In other words, Koreans consider red color as warm and burning, while they think of blue color as cold and freezing. Therefore, they use red color when referring to being in debt, whereas they use red color when referring to going up of stock index. We often find such incoherence in the newspaper articles, but people do not confuse the meaning due to the different kind of experiential basis. The conceptual metaphor SIGNAL IS A COLOR is also found in our everyday lives. In the traffic lights, colored lights control and direct traffic. In the same way, signal lights operate in our daily lives. The red light means warning or danger, the yellow light represents waiting, and the green light stands for permission or hope.

Let us consider the following expressions.

    (13) a. *See the red light*

        b. The government *gave the green light* to the minister's

           plans for reducing unemployment.

See the red light in (13a) means seeing possible danger in the future. The sino-Korean word *cekshinho* 'a red light' also refers to a danger signal. The red sign represents the stop signal in the traffic light, and it means a dangerous signal in everyday expression as well. The conceptual metaphor DANGER IS RED exists in our conceptual system.

The color *green* is the customary sign in the traffic lights that there is no danger present and that one may therefore continue on one's way. Accordingly, *to give the green light* in (13b) means giving permission to someone to do something. *To get the green light* is a similar expression. In Korean, *chengshinho* 'blue or green signal' refers to a good signal for something because it means permission. The sino-Korean word *cheng* is the color term covering both blue and green. Here, also, the conceptual metaphor PERMISSION OR SAFETY IS GREEN governs our conceptual system.

The following example is from a Korean daily newspaper (*The Chosun Ilbo*, August 9, 2000).

    (14) "*mi kumli phalan −pwul,*

        (lit.) U.S.A. interest-rate blue light,

(int.) The interest-rate of U.S.A. shows a hopeful signal,

　　yuka ppalgan −pwul,

(lit.) oil price red light,

(int.) the oil price indicates a dangerous signal,

　　pantochey　　　　　cwu nolan −pwul"

(lit.) semiconductor stocks yellow light

(int.) the semiconductor stocks show a waiting signal.

Experiential basis of different kinds is found in the following examples which are often seen in the newspaper.

(15) a. *ol swuchwul mokphyo −ey ppalkan pwul*

　　　this year export goal−Loc red light

　　　(lit.) red light on this year export goal

　　　(int.) dangerous signal on the export goal of this year

　b. *kaykcang −uy cenkwangphan −i onthong ppalkan pwul*

　　　floor−Gen electric bulletin board−Nom entirely red light

　　　(lit.) the electric bulletin board of the floor is entirely red

　　　(int.) the electric bulletin board (of a security company floor) is entirely covered with red light because almost all stock prices go up

The red lights of (15a) and (15b) have contrastive meanings, one is negative and the other is positive. In other words, (15a) is based on the conceptual metaphor SIGNAL IS A COLOR, and (15b) is based on the conceptual metaphor TEMPERATURE IS A COLOR.

The fact that those who read newspapers understand their meaning without confusing shows the conceptual metaphors are part of our conceptual system.

In addition, red letters sometimes mean important things we must remember, so generally students write down important things in red on their textbooks. However, red letters sometimes refer to something to avoid in Korean. Generally, Korean people do not like their names written in red, and they forbid children to write people's names in red.

In addition to the above conceptual metaphors, the color *red* has a lot of implications which mostly come from metonymies because it gives people a strong impression.

> (16) a. It was *a red-letter day* for us when Paul came here.
>
> b. We will have to get out *the red carpet* when such an important person comes to visit us.
>
> c. Although official censorship ended in Russia some years ago, *red tape* can still shackle film-makers working there.
>
> d. He *drew a red herring across her path.*
>
> e. The prime minister tried to tell the country that there were *reds under the beds*, that the miners were infiltrated with communists.

Red-letter day in (16a) means a specially happy day that will be remembered. Red letters on the calendar mean that they are important days on which something good or special happens. People feel happy to see red letters on the calendar because we can have rest on those days. *Red carpet* in (16b) means a special ceremonial welcome to a guest, so *red* represents being important or being royal.

From the fact that red tape is used to bind official papers in government departments, the idiom *red tape* in (16c) means the heavy use of and emphasis on official papers, formal details, rules, etc. But most Korean people do not understand the meaning of *red tape*. They consider *red tape* as an illegal and lewd film. To them *red* stands for something lascivious and pornographic.

The idiom *draw a red herring across someone's path* in (16d) can be interpreted only when we know the property of a red herring: it is a type of fish that has a smell strong enough to confuse hunting dogs. The expression *a red herring* is used to mean a suggestion or a piece of information introduced into a situation in order to draw someone's attention away from the truth or more important part of the situation. These idioms may be difficult to understand to people whose culture does not contain herring or hunting.

When *red* means communism, both metonymy and metaphor are related to it. It may begin with metonymy as suggested in the fact that communists usually wore red arm-bands. While the color *red* stands for communism, the color *white* does anti-communism. It seems that people tend to understand abstract ideology in terms of concrete colors like *red* or *white*. Therefore, the conceptual metaphor IDEOLOGY IS A COLOR shapes our language and thought. *Reds under the beds* in (33d) represents members of the communist party. *The Red Army* refers to the communist troops of USSR and *Red China* represents the communist China in contrast to Taiwan. In the same way, *red* is used to indicate something in relation with communism in Korean. *Ppalgayngi* (lit. 'a red guy') is a derogatory name referring to a communist. The sino-Korean word *cekhwa* (lit. 'red becoming') means communization. The term 'red complex' was on a recent newspaper, and people understand that *red* means communism.

The conceptual metaphor PEOPLE ARE PLANTS is related with the color term *green* and *yellow*. When the color of plants is green, it means that the plants are young or not old, so that the color *green* metaphorically means both inexperience and vitality of a person.

> (17) a. When she left school and started her first job, she was
>   *as green as grass*.
>   b. When he bought the house everybody thought he was
>   wasting his money. But he's not *as green as he's
>   cabbage-looking*—that part of town is now very
>   fashionable, and his house is worth far more than he
>   paid for it.
>   c. a man in his *green old age*
>   d. White paper *yellows with age*.
>   (cf. The leaves of the trees begin to yellow in autumn.)

As green as grass in (17a) represents lacking experience of the world or of life, and *be not as green as one is cabbage-looking* in (17b) means being not as foolish or inexperienced as one looks. Inexperienced persons may be credulous as suggested in *a green hand* or *a green man*. In a positive sense, the color *green* stands for

80

vitality or youth as in (17c), which means a vigorous and active old man. In (17d), paper is personified and the color *yellow* represents an old person.

The following examples are from Korean.

(18) a. *cheng −chwun*

(lit.) green spring

(int.) the springtime of life or the heyday of youth

b. *sayphalahkey celm −un kes −i mues −ul anu −nya*

green−like young one−Nom what−Acc know−Inter

(lit.) What does a green-like young one know

(int.) What does a very young one know?

c. *phwus −kwail, phwusnaki*

unripe fruits, inexperienced person

d. *ssakswu −ka nolahta*

hope−Nom be.yellow

(lit.) hope or promise is yellow

(int.) there is no future

The prefix *phwus-* in (18c) means something green, unripe, inexperienced or fresh, so they are the concepts which the color term *green* reminds people of. In addition, the prefix *phwus-* is attached to both plants and persons as seen in (18c), which indicates that the conceptual metaphor PEOPLE ARE PLANTS is part of our conceptual system. (18d) reminds people that yellow, but not green, leaves do not grow well.

The color term *green* has other senses as suggested in the following.

(19) a. He has always *had green fingers*, so it is not surprising that they have a beautiful garden.

b. As the sea became rougher and the boat rolled from side to side, many passengers began to look *green about the gills*.

From the fact that plants have the color, *green* means growing plants or flowers. It is a kind of metonymy, a cause−effect metonymy. *To have green fingers* in (19a) means having an ability to grow plants and flowers. It is the color of growing plants, so that it reminds people of freshness. Freshness means being strong and full of life as in *green memory*. On the other hand, the color term *green* can also refer to unhealthily pale color in the face from sickness, fear, etc. In (19b) *green about the gills* means looking as though one were about to be sick or vomit. If *white* is used instead of *green*, it means showing signs of terror rather than sickness.

In Korean, the green color usually has positive meanings. The Korean terms *phalahta* or *phwuluta* covers both green and blue. It reminds people of woods, freshness, permission and environment campaign. Therefore, many Korean students have difficulty in understanding the meaning like (19b) at first unless they learn about them. In an experiment which I conducted for this study,[13] no subject guessed the correct meaning of *green-eyed*. The Korean students guessed that *a green eye* means peacefulness rather than envy.

Yellow constitutes a relatively small number of idioms.

---

13) The details of the experiment will be reported in Chapter 4.

> (20) a. They are *too yellow to fight*.
>
>   b. *yellow press*

Yellow in (20a) means coward or not brave. This usage is not familiar to Korean students, so they didn't make a good guess of it in the experiment mentioned above. (20b) refers to newspapers that try to make all matters exciting rather than reporting them exactly. Sometimes Korean *nolahta* 'yellow' may also represent lasciviousness.[14]

In Korean, *nolahta* has both positive and negative concepts. It may remind brightness, but it is used negatively in some idioms.

> (21) a. *nolangi*
>
>   (lit.) a yellow one
>
>   (int.) a stingy person
>
>   b. *elkwul —i nolahta*
>
>   face—Nom be.yellow
>
>   (lit.) (Someone's) face is yellow.
>
>   (int.) Someone looks poor, someone has sickness like jaundice.

Yellow in (21a) conveys the meaning of stinginess, and (21b) refers to yellowish face by poverty or sickness like jaundice.

Blue has meanings which appear to be unrelated to one another.

---

14) The following expression is in *The Dong — a Ilbo* on 27, November, 2000.
    yocum yenyey phulo — nun onthong 'nolan sayk'
    nowadays amusement program—Top entirely 'yellow color'
    (lit.) Nowadays amusement programs are entirely yellow
    (int.) Amusement programs of these days are entirely lascivious.

Most expressions with *blue* come from metonymy. Let us consider the following expressions:

> (22) a. He just arrived *out of the blue*.
>
> b. I had only recently seen my friend in a restaurant. The news of his death came as *a bolt from the blue*.
>
> c. He is a *blue-collar* worker.
>
> d. *boys in blue*
>
> e. *blue-coat*
>
> f. He has *blue blood* in his veins.
>
> g. The shares of this company are *blue chip*.
>
> h. You can depend on him for help whenever you're in trouble. He's a *true blue*.

Blue is the color of sky; in the idioms like *out of a (clear) blue sky* and *out of the blue*, which mean 'unexpectedly,' are based on the color of sky. *A bolt from the blue* in (22b) has the similar meaning. It means something completely unexpected, originally referring to lightning suddenly coming from the sky. Likewise, Korean has a sino-Korean word *cheng −chen −pyeklyek* 'blue sky thunderbolt' which has the same meaning as 'a bolt from the blue'.

From the blue color of clothes, *blue-collar* workers represents those who do physical or dirty work with their hands, which is contrasted with *white-collar*. *Boys in blue* in (22d) represents men of the police force, referring to the blue uniform. Similarly, *blue-coat* in (22e) refers to police officers from their clothes.

Like *green, blue* also represents paleness such as *blue in the face*.

84

In Korean, *blue* means paleness when it is used with a person's face, whereas it means turning green with leaves or plants. The reason is Korean *phalay −cita* covers both green and blue.[15)]

In (22f) and (22g), *blue* represents superiority or excellence. *Blue blood* of (22f) means the blood of a noble or royal family, which is a translation of Spanish *sagre azul* used by some families to mean that their blood was pure Spanish and that they had no Moorish blood. According to *Longman Dictionary of English Idioms* (1979), the phrase perhaps refers to the blue color of the veins of people who have light skin. In Korean, blue color represents coolness or coldness in contrast with *red*,[16)] so that many people do not understand the meaning of *blue blood*. They may guess it means a cold-hearted person or a cold-blooded animal. Actually more than 30% of the Korean students who were given the question answered that they think it represents cruelty or cold-heartedness, while no one answered correctly.

---

15) The examples are like the following:
   a. elkwul −i phalay −cita
      face −Nom blue −become
      (lit.) (Someone's) face becomes blue.
      (int.) Someone's face turns pale.
   b. phalah −key cilyess −ta
      blue −like be overawed −Past
      (lit.) (Someone) was overawed with blue color.
      (int.) (Someone) turned deadly pale (with horror).
   c. namuiph −i phalay −cita
      leaves −Nom green −become
      (lit.) Leaves become green.
      (int.) Leaves of trees turn green.
16) The conceptual metaphor TEMPERATURE IS A COLOR (HOTNESS IS RED, COLDNESS IS BLUE) is mentioned earlier.

Blue chip in (22g) means a share that is costly and of good quality. It is widely used in the Korean stock market as a loan-word.

True blue in (22h) means a loyal trustworthy person, perhaps originally referring to the unchanging color of the sky. Sometimes *true blue* represents being stubborn or strict as an adjective or such a person as a noun.

2. Body—Part Term Idioms

Our body is often used to represent the concepts of place or location perhaps because our body is the object which we experience most often and which is the most convenient standpoint of indicating relative locations. Across many languages in the world, body-part terms have been developed into adpositions to represent locative relations, which reveals the pattern of conceptual shift that one meaning is changed into another in our conceptual knowledge. Metaphoric shift is necessary in this process. In many languages, according to Heine (1997: 41−49), words denoting *back* and *head* have been shifted to represent the concept *above*, while words denoting *breast / chest, face* and *mouth* have been changed to represent *front*. Heine (1997: 137) suggests common transfer patterns from body-part terms to abstract schemas, as in Table 7.

Table 7. Some common transfer patterns from body-part terms to abstract schema

Source	Target
'Head'	'top end', 'tip'
'Buttocks', 'foot'	'bottom end'
'Mouth'	'opening', 'edge'
'Neck', 'wrist'	'narrow section'

Language is influenced by culture; thus, a language reflects many aspects of the culture in which the language is used. Idioms are a part of a language. Therefore, some idioms have common meanings across cultures, while others are different from culture to culture.

In this section, I will study some body-part term idioms based on common conceptual metaphors in English and Korean such as *head, hand,* and *face,* and idioms without common conceptual metaphors in English and Korean like *nose, liver,* and *heart.* In English, many idioms are motivated by conceptual metaphors or metonymies. Many Korean idioms are also based on some conceptual metaphors or metonymies. What is more interesting is that some body part terms represent certain concepts with coherence. The contrastive analysis between English and Korean idioms, which presents their similarities and differences, will help Korean students learning English to understand and learn some English idioms.

1) Idioms with Common Conceptual Metaphors between English and Korean

In this section, I will explore common conceptual metaphors and metonymies which underlie both English and Korean body-part term idioms. When there are common conceptual metaphors between English and Korean, Korean students learning English tend to learn English idioms more easily than the cases without common conceptual metaphors.[17]

HEAD

Let us consider the following examples:

> (23) a. I have boasted in my youth and *held my head high* and gone on my way careless of consequences.
>
> b. Before his trial he was ashamed to be seen in public, but now that he has been proved not guilty he can *hold his head up* once more.
>
> c. His *head is swollen* since he won a prize for his poetry.
>
> d. the *head* waiter
>
> e. the *head* of the department

The italicized expressions in (23a−b) mean 'to erect one's head,' which represents being arrogant, and a *swollen head* like (23c) and *a*

---

17) The details of the experiment will be reported in Chapter 4.

big head refer to the belief that someone is very clever or more important than one really is. In (23d−e), *head* refers to a chief person or a thing in the highest position. These expressions are based on the conceptual metaphor HAVING CONTROL OR FORCE IS UP; BEING SUBJECT TO CONTROL OR FORCE IS DOWN.

Korean also has the same conceptual metaphor. The two Korean terms *meli* and *kokay* correspond to one English term *head*. As a body part term, *kokay* means the back of a neck or the upper part of a neck. When it is used to indicate the upper part of a neck, most idioms including it imply a person's reputation or prestige. Examples are as follows:

(24) a. *kokay −lul ttelkwu −ta*

    head−Acc drop

    (lit.) to drop one's head

    (int.) 'to droop, to lose heart'

  b. *kokay −ka swukuleci −ta*

    head−Nom become low

    (lit.) Someone's head becomes low.

    (int.) 'Respecting mind comes into being in itself.'

  c. *kokay −lul swuki −ta*

    head−Acc lower

    (lit.) to lower one's head

    (int.) 'to apologize'

  d. *kokay −lul swukuli −ta*

    head−Acc lower

    (lit.) to lower one's head

       (int.) 'to have one's spirits dampened'

  e. *kokay −lul mos −tul −ta*

     head − Acc not raise

     (lit.) not to raise one's head

     (int.) 'to feel shameful'

  f. *kokay −lul ppassppassi seywu −ta*

     head − Acc firmly make stand

     (lit.) to hold out one's head stiffly

     (int.) 'to erect one's head'

These idioms have the same meaning though *kokay* is replaced by *meli*. We take the above expressions as a matter of course because the conceptual metaphor organizes our conceptual system. Like (23d −e), Korean *meli*, but not *kokay*, represents the highest person of a group, as in (25).

  (25) *wudwu −meli nolus −ul hata*

      boss role − Acc do

      (lit.) to do boss's role

      (int.) 'to play a part of chief'

English *head* and Korean *meli* represent a part at the top of an object which is separate from the body. Especially, Korean *meli* can be attached to the end of a word in order to represent the top or the front part of something. Increasingly the meaning of top or front part of something disappears and *meli* is considered as a suffix without special meaning.

(26) a. the *head* of a hammer, the *head* of the nail

b. *kidwung −meli* 'the top part of a pillar'

c. *papsang −meli* 'the front part of a dining table'

Furthermore, *head* and *meli* refer to the beginning of something as in (27).

(27) a. the *head* of the letter

b. I waited at the *head* of the line.

c. *mal −meli*

speech head

'the beginning part of speech'

d. *ches −meli*

first head

'the beginning part of something.'

e. *yen −dwu kica hoykyen* (sino-Korean expression)

year −head press interview

'the New Year's press interview'

f. *modwu −uy han kwucel*

the opening paragraph −Gen one passage

'one of the opening paragraph'

The word *meli* has various meanings like 'head', 'brain', 'hair' or 'ideas'. Meanings of *meli* include those of *kokay,* so that most idioms with *kokay* can be replaced by idioms including *meli* without any noticeable meaning change. But some idioms including *meli* are not replaced by idioms including *kokay,* Physically *meli* represents the part which includes brain or the upper part of a neck. *Kokay* does not represent brain or hair, and *kokay* has more physical meaning than *meli*. The following expressions cannot be replaced by the expressions with *kokay*, which means *kokay* is used to represent the physical part of head.

    (28) a. *meli −ka kapyep −ta*

         head −Nom be.light

         (lit.) Someone's head is light.

         (int.) 'to feel refreshing'

      b. *meli −ka mukep −ta*

         head −Nom be.heavy

         (lit.) Someone's head is heavy.

         (int.) 'Someone's head feels heavy, someone is in low spirits.'

In the examples in (29), *meli* refers to the physical part, so that *kokay* is also used instead of *meli*.

    (29) a. *meli −lul tul −ta*

         head −Acc raise

         (lit.) to raise one's head

         (int.) 'Some ideas occur to head or something becomes known.'

      b. *meli −lul naymil −ta*

         head −Acc hold out

         (lit.) to hold out one's head

         (int.) 'to make an appearance'

The expressions in (29) have the meaning of appearance. When something appears, usually the head comes first. Meanwhile, there is a case in which *meli* has the same meaning as but is less used than *kokay* when referring to a body part as in (30).

(30) *kokay −lul tolli −ta*

head − Acc turn

(lit.) to turn away one's head

(int.) 'to turn away one's face, not to see something anymore'

A head is one of the most important parts of a body, so that the English phrase *headline news* and Korean *meli −kisa* refer to main points of news. Similarly, in the phrase *the head of the table*, the *head* means the most important place.

Metonymically English *head* and Korean *meli* can mean life. Examples are suggested in (31).

(31) a. *for one's head* 'for one's life'

b. *meli −lul nay −noh −ala*[18] (usually in the discourse of bandits)

head − Acc put out − Imp

(lit.) put out your head

(int.) 'give me your head(life)'

People think that they see a certain person even when they see only his / her face, and the head includes face, so that the head

---

18) In Korean, *mok* 'neck' is also used to refer to someone's life.

stands for the entire body. The following expressions illustrate such a metonymic extension.

(32) a. *crowned heads* 'crowned persons＝king and queen'
   b. *wise heads* 'wise persons'
   c. *meli −ka khu −ta*
      head−Nom be.big
      (lit.) head is big
      (int.) 'to become an adult'

Animals or people are also counted by counting their heads, as illustrated in (33).

(33) a. *fifty heads of cattle*
   b. *charge $2 a head*

Korean also expresses the number of cattles by the sino-Korean word *dwu* representing *meli*.

(34) a. *sayuk dwu swu −ka kamso −hata*
      breeding head number−Nom decrease
      (lit.) the number of breeding head decreases
      (int.) 'The number of breeding cattles decreases.'
   b. *in −dwu −sey*
      person head tax
      (lit.) a person head tax
      (int.) 'a poll tax'

94

c. *dwu —dang paykman —won*

head per a million won

(lit.) one million won per head

(int.) 'one million won per person'

Head includes brain, and brain stands for intelligence or ability.

(35) a. *have a head for* 'to be clever at something'

b. *get into one's head* 'to make someone or oneself understand'

c. *above someone's head, over someone's head*

'beyond someone's understanding, too difficult'

d. He has *an old head on young shoulders.*

'the sensible behaviour of an experienced person'

(36) a. *meli —lul mou —ta*

head — Acc get together

(lit.) to get together heads

(int.) 'to put opinions together'

b. *meli —lul ssu —ta*

head — Acc use

(lit.) to use head

(int.) 'to use one's brain (head)'

c. *meli —ka coh —ta*

head — Nom be.good

(lit.) to have a good head

(int.) 'to be clever'

d. *meli —ka nappu —ta*

head — Nom be.bad

(lit.) to have a bad head

(int.) 'to have a poor head'

e. *meli −ka iss −ta*

head − Nom exist

(lit.) head is existent

(int.) 'to have brains, to be sensible'

f. *meli −ka eps −ta*

head − Nom not exist

(lit.) head is not existent

(int.) 'to have no brains (sense)'

g. *meli −lul sikhi −ta*

head − Acc cool off

'to cool one's head'

A person's head also controls him or her, so that *head* represents senses or reason in the following idioms: *lose one's head* 'to act wildly or without reason', *keep one's head* 'to remain calm', *keep a level head* 'to be calm, sensible, and able to judge well in difficult situations', *off one's head* 'out of one's senses', and *an old head on young shoulders* '(a young person who has) the sensible behaviour of an experienced person'. If head stands for reason, then heart does emotion, as illustrated in (37).

(37) Her heart rules her head.

'Her emotion rules her reason.'

Korean has similar expressions like (38).

(38) *mitum −un meli −lo ka anila kasum −ulo hanun kes −ita*

     faith −Top head −Inst not breast −Inst doing thing be

     (lit.) faith is the thing which is done by not head but breast

     (int.) 'Faith is the thing which is done by not reason but heart.'

What is interesting in Korean is that *meli* is used to designate hair. In (39a − c), *meli* refers to hair.

(39) a. *meli −lul kkakk −ta*

       hair − Acc cut

       (lit.) to cut someone's hair

       (int.) 'to have one's hair cut'

     b. *meli −lul ecn −ta*

       hair − Acc put on top

       (lit.) to put up one's hair

       (int.) '(a woman) gets married'

     c. *meli −lul phwul −ta*

       hair − Acc loosen

       (lit.) to loosen one's hair

       (int.) 'to go into mourning'

(39a) has three meanings. The first meaning is to have a haircut, the second one is becoming a monk, and the last one is being in prison. The second and the third meanings develop metonymically from the act of haircut when a person becomes a monk or a prisoner. (39b) and (39c) reflect special Korean customs. (39b) means '(a woman) is married to (a man),' which reflects the old customs of changing hair styles at marriage. (39c) represents an old custom of loosening a person's hair when being in a mourning.

To sum up, English and Korean idioms related with *head* have many shared properties. English *head* and Korean *meli* or *kokay* are used based on the conceptual metaphor HAVING CONTROL OR FORCE IS UP; BEING SUBJECT TO CONTROL OR FORCE IS DOWN. Metonymically, English *head* and Korean *meli* represent a person or an animal, and both of them stand for a person's intelligence. But Korean *meli* stands for hair metonymically, and it can be used as a suffix.

HAND

Hands are useful parts of our body. People use hands to do something; thus, in English *hand* metonymically represents a person, working especially with hands. In Korean, *son* 'hand' also refers to a person who can help with hands as illustrated in (40). They are the cases of the metonymy BODY PART FOR THE PERSON, which is a special case of the metonymy THE PART FOR THE WHOLE.

> (40) a. *farm hands, factory hands*
>
>   b. *all hands on board*
>
>   c. *son −i ttalli −ta {pucokha −ta, mocala −ta}*
>
>   hand −Nom lack
>
>   (lit.) to be short of hands
>
>   (int.) 'to be short of working persons'
>
>   d. *son −i manh −ta*
>
>   hand −Nom be.many

(lit.) there are many hands

(int.) 'there are plenty of persons to work'

Korean *son* can refer to fingers in hands, too. It is also a kind of metonymy and examples in (41) are cases of the metonymy THE WHOLE FOR THE PART.

(41) a. *son kkopa heyali −ta*

hand counting count

(lit.) using one's fingers count

(int.) 'to count with fingers'

b. *son −i kop −ta*

hand −Nom be.numb

(lit.) hand is numb

(int.) 'Someone's fingers are stiff with the cold.'

Both in English and Korean, *hand* refers to skill of hands. In (42a), *an old hand* means a person with long experience by adding *old* to *a hand* which stands for both a person and skill. *Hand* refers to a practitioner of a skill, so that it is also a kind of the metonymy BODY PART FOR THE PERSON. (43) shows that Korean *son* also stands for skill or hand-touch; thus, Korean has the metonymy CONTROLLER FOR CONTROLLED in this case.

(42) a. *an old hand*

b. I'm *a bad hand* at making pastry.

(43) a. *son −i kechil −ta*

     hand −Nom be.rough

     (lit.) Someone's hand is rough.

     (int.) 'to be not skillful'

  b. *son −i mayp −ta*

     hand −Nom be.hot

     (lit.) Someone's hand is hot.

     (int.) 'Someone's hand-touch is severe.'

  c. *son −i yemul −ta*

     hand −Nom get ripe

     (lit.) Someone's hand gets ripe.

     (int.) 'The result of doing something with hands is good.'

  d. *son(−i)*[19] *sethwulu −ta*

     hand(−Nom) be.unskilled

     (lit.) Someone's hand is unskilled.

     (int.) 'to be a poor hand at something'

  e. *son(−ey) ik −ta {ikswukha −ta}*

     hand(−Loc) be.skilled

     (lit.) to be skilled to hands

     (int.) 'to get skillful'

Moreover, *son* refers to a habitual action of hands, a blow or strike which is done with hands. It is also a kind of the metonymy CONTROLLER FOR CONTROLLED.

---

19) The parenthesis means that the idiom can be used without the particle in the parenthesis.

100

    (44) *son −i kechil −ta*

    hand − Nom be.rough

    (lit.) Someone's hand is rough.

    (int.) 'to be light of fingers, to be thievish'

    (45) a. *son(−ul) tay −ta*

        hand(− Acc) touch

        (lit.) to touch with hands

        (int.) 'to give a blow to someone'

    b. *sonccikem(−ul) ha −ta*

        hand − striking(− Acc) do

        (lit.) to do striking with hands

        (int.) 'to strike a person with hands'

(44) is an example of a habitual action of hands and (45) is an expression meaning a blow or strike which is done with hands. In the above examples in (45), particles in parentheses mean that idioms are used without the particles. In many colloquial expressions, usage without particles is more usual and natural.

In English, *hand* refers to handwriting in *write a clear hand*, and it means applause in *a big hand*. Handwriting and applause belong to manual activities; thus, they are examples of the metonymy CONTROLLER FOR CONTROLLED. Unlike English *hand*, Korean *son* does not mean handwriting, and it does not mean applause alone, but it has the meaning applause with other words such as *sonppyek* and *pakswu*[20]

---

20) *pakswu (sino-Korean)*
    clap hand
    'hand clapping'

'handclapping.' Instead, Korean *son* represents handling care as in (46) and manual activities as in (47).

(46) a. *son(−ul) po −ta*

    hand(− Acc) see

    (lit.) to take charge of something with hands

    (int.) 'to see to it (that there are no defects)'

  b. *son(−i) manhi ka −ta*

    hand(− Nom) much go

    (lit.) Hand is much required.

    (int.) 'to require much work'

(47) a. *son(−i) ttu −ta*

    hand(− Nom) be.slow

    (lit.) Hand is slow.

    (int.) 'Manual movements are too slow.'

  b. *son(−i) ssa −ta*

    hand(− Nom) be.swift

    (lit.) Hand is swift.

    (int.) 'Manual movements are fast.'

  c. *son(−ul) memchwu −ta*

    hand(− Acc) stop

    (lit.) to stop hands

    (int.) 'to stop doing something'

  d. *son(−ul) noh −ta*

    hand(− Acc) take off

    (lit.) to take off hands

102

(int.) ① 'to let go one's hold of'

② 'to give up one's work'

③ 'to release'

e. *son(−ul) tay −ta*

hand(−Acc) touch

(lit.) to touch with hands

(int.) ① 'to touch'

② 'to strike'

③ 'to correct'

④ 'to embezzle others' money

f. *son(−ul) tha −ta*

hand(−Acc) be.sensitive

(lit.) to be sensitive to hands

(int.) ① 'to be sensitive to handling'

② 'to be lost through handling'

g. *son(−ul) tul −ta*

hand(−Acc) raise

(lit.) to raise hands

(int.) ① 'to raise one's hand'

② 'to be beaten, to yield'

③ 'to be floored, to be annoyed'

h. *son(−i) pwukkulep −ta*

hand(−Nom) be.ashamed

(lit.) Hand is ashamed.

(int.) 'to be embarrassed by nonfulfillment of a request
for which one has extended one's hand'

Metaphorically, English *hand* represents possession, assistance, control, and responsibility, which are related with the role of hands. For instance, hands are always used to help someone, so that help or aid is represented by the hand. In the following examples, (48a−b) represents possession; (48c−d) refers to assistance.

(48) a. *fall into someone's hands* 'to come into the power of'
   b. *change hands* 'to go from the possession of one person to that of another'
   c. *give / lend a hand* 'to help or assist'
   d. *hold one's hand* 'to give support to someone at a difficult time'

Korean has the same metaphors, possession and assistance, as in (49) and (50).

(49) a. *nam −uy son −ey neme −ka −ta*
   others−Gen hand−Loc be passed on
   (lit.) to be passed on others' hands
   (int.) 'to fall into others'
   b. *nam −uy son −ey tteleci −ta*
   others−Gen hand−Loc fall
   (lit.) to fall into others' hands
   (int.) 'to fall into others'
   c. *son −ey neh −ta*
   hand−Loc put in
   (lit.) to put something into hands

(int.) 'to get, to obtain'

d. *son −ey cwi −ta*

hand−Loc take hold of

(lit.) to take hold of something in hands

(int.) 'to take possession of something'

e. *son(−ul) thel −ta*

hand(−Acc) empty

(lit.) to empty hands

(int.) 'to lose all the capital'

(50) a. *son(−ul) pil −ta*

hand(−Acc) borrow

(lit.) to borrow hands

(int.) 'to ask (a person) a helping hand'

b. *son(−ul) pwa −cwu −ta*

hand(−Acc) look after

(lit.) to look after someone or something with hands

(int.) ① 'to give (a person) a helping hand'

② 'to give (a person) a hard time' (a slang in gangsters)

People can control something with hands, so that English has many idioms with *hand* meaning control, as in (51).

(51) a. You've been very badly behaved recently. I can see I shall have to *take* you *in hand.*

b. Since you left, things at the factory have got completely

> *out of hand.*
> c. He rules this place *with a very heavy hand.*
> d. This is going to be a particularly tough and confusing day at work, mainly because associates and colleagues are trying to *get the upper hand.*
> e. The statesman *held* the fate of his country *in the palm of his hand.*

The word *hand* in (51) may be replaced by *control* without any meaning change, though such expressions are not idiomatic. The idiom in (51a) means taking a person or thing under control especially to try to make improvements. *Out of hand* in (51b) represents out of control, and *with a heavy hand* in (51c) means with firm control. *The upper hand* in (51d) stands for the position of power or control.

Korean has similar expressions meaning control as in the following.

(52) a. *ku −il −un nay son an −ey iss −ta*
the matter −Top my hand inside −Loc exist
(lit.) The matter is in my hand.
(int.) 'The matter is in my control.'

b. *ttwie −pwa −ya puchenim son −patak i −ta*
run try −though Buddha hand −palm is
(lit.) Though we try to run, we are in the Buddha's hand −palm.
(int.) Though we try to run away, we are in the Buddha's control.

People do many things with hands and therefore *hand* may mean responsibility or connection in English, as shown in (53). Korean *son* is also used meaning connection rather than responsibility, as in (54).

(53) a. I have a great deal or work *on my hands*

    b. Now that the children are *off my hands*, I have more free time.

    c. If you're going to regard every suggestion I make as a criticism, I will *wash my hands of* the whole matter.

    d. Why didn't you tell me if you *had a hand in* the bank job?

(54) a. *son(−ul) tay −ta*

    hand(−Acc) touch

    (lit.) to touch with hands

    (int.) 'to put out one's hands' → 'to start'

    b. *son(−ul) ttey −ta*

    hand(−Acc) take off

    (lit.) to take off hands

    (int.) 'to withdraw oneself from something'

    c. *son(−ul) kkunh −ta*

    hand(−Acc) cut off

    (lit.) to cut off hands

    (int.) 'to cut oneself from something' → 'to break off'

    d. *son(−ul) ppay −ta*

    hand(−Acc) take out

    (lit.) to take out hands

    (int.) 'to take out one's hands of' → 'to evade'

    e. *son(−ul) ssiss −ta*

      hand(−Acc) wash

      (lit.) to wash hands

      (int.) 'to wash hands' → 'to break off'

    f. *son(−ul) cap −ta*

      hand(−Acc) grasp

      (lit.) to grasp hands

      (int.) 'to join hands with, to reconcile with'

The idioms in (53a) and (53b) represent responsibility, (53c) means both responsibility and connection, and (53d) represents connection. *Wash one's hands of* in (53c) is very similar to the Korean example (54e). In addition, (54b), (54c), (54d) and (54e) have the same meaning in many cases.

Korean *son* refers to a way or means to do something as in (55), and English *hand* has such idioms as *try one's hand* 'to attempt'.

    (55) *son(−ul) ssu −ta*

      hand(−Acc) use

      (lit.) to use hands

      (int.) 'to try every possible means'

Korean *son* has peculiar meanings such as liberality or generosity as in (56), and English *hand* is used similarly in the expression *with an open hand* 'in a generous way'.

(56) *son(−i) khu −ta*

    hand(−Nom) be.big

    (lit.) hands are big

    (int.) 'to be free with one's money, to be extravagantly generous'

English *hand* and Korean *son* share many things in their meanings. They show such metonymy as BODY PART FOR THE PERSON and CONTROLLER FOR CONTROLLED. But Korean *son* is used to represent more various handling care and manual activities than English *hand*. Metaphorically both English *hand* and Korean *son* represent possession, help, control, responsibility and connection.

FACE

In general people judge a person from his / her face. When they take a look at a picture of a person's face, they consider that they have seen the picture of the person. In other words, as Lakoff and Johnson (1980: 37) indicate, people perceive a person in terms of his or her face and act on those perceptions. Therefore, a person's face represents the person metonymically. This metonymy is THE FACE FOR THE PERSON, which is a special case of the metonymy THE PART FOR THE WHOLE. Two Korean words *nach* and *elkwul* correspond to the English word *face*. *Nach and elkwul* have almost the same meaning, so that in many cases of expressions *elkwul* can replace *nach*, and vice versa.[21] The examples of metonymy are shown in (57).

---

21) But *nach* can be attached to other adjectives or verbs. The idioms including *nach* are usually used without particles like −*i*, or −*ul*. In my opinion the partial reason is that *nach* is one syllable word like *son* in Korean.

(57) a. show one's face 'appear'

    b. *elkwul −ul poi −ta*

       face − Acc show

       (int.) 'to show up, to make one's appearance'

    c. *elkwul −ul naymil −ta*

       face − Acc thrust out

       (lit.) to thrust out one's face

       (int.) 'to show up'

    d. *elkwul −i phalli −ta*

       *f*ace − Nom become sold

       (lit.) Someone's face becomes sold.

       (int.) 'Someone becomes known (to people).'

Both English *face* and Korean *nach* or *elkwul* mean appearance or visage of a person, but Korean *nach* or *elkwul* are not used to inanimate things unlike English *face* which also has such meaning as the front or surface of something. Korean examples are illustrated in (58).

(58) a. *elkwul −i panpanha −ta*

       face − Nom be.handsome

       (lit.) Someone's face is handsome.

       (int.) 'Someone is pretty.'

    b. *elkwul −i phi −ta*

       face − Nom bloom

       (lit.) Someone's face blooms.

       (int.) 'Someone looks better.'

    c. *elkwul kaps −ul ha −ta*

face value−Acc do

(lit.) to do one's face value

(int.) 'to exploit one's beauty'

A person's face represents a person and it singles out the person among others. Korean *nach* or *elkwul* represents familiarity, as in (59).

(59) a. *nach −i (elkwul −i) ik −ta*

face−Nom be.ripe

(lit.) Someone's face is ripe.

(int.) 'Someone is familiar.'

b. *nach −i sel −ta*

face−Nom be.unripe

(lit.) Someone's face is unripe.

(int.) 'Someone is unfamiliar.'

c. *nach −ul kali −ta*

face−Acc distinguish

(lit.) to distinguish faces

(int.) 'to show preferences'

The most important and the most frequent metaphorical meaning of English *face* and Korean *nach* or *elkwul* is a person's reputation or honor, because people judge a person from the face and face has the function of seeing, hearing, speaking and thinking. The conceptual metaphor HONOR IS A FACE is involved in our thought and our lives. (60a−b) and (61a−h) show English and Korean examples, respectively.

(60) a. When he failed to beat his opponent he felt he had *lost face* with his friends, who all expected him to win.

   b. After all his failures, the win *saved his face*.

(61) a. *nach −ul (elkwul −ul) kkakk −ta*

   face − Acc cut

   (lit.) to cut one's face

   (int.) 'to impair one's honor'

   b. *nach −i kkakki −ta*

   face − Nom be cut

   (lit.) Someone's face is cut.

   (int.) 'to lose one's face'

   c. *nach −ul seywu −ta*

   face − Acc make stand

   (lit.) to erect one's face

   (int.) 'to save one's face'

   d. *nach −ey (elkwul −ey) ttongchilha −ta*

   face − Loc smear with dung

   (lit.) to smear one's face with dung

   (int.) 'to ruin one's honor'

   e. *nach −ul (elkwul −ul) mostul −ta*

   face − Acc not raise

   (lit.) not to raise one's face

   (int.) 'to be ashamed of oneself'

   f. *nach −i (elkwul −i) kancilep −ta*

   face − Nom tickle

   (lit.) Someone's face tickles.

        (int.) 'to be ashamed'

g. *nach −i (elkwul −i) twukkep −ta*

   face −Nom be.thick

   (lit.) Someone's face is thick.

   (int.) 'Someone is impudent or shameless'

h. *elkwul −ey chelpan −ul kkal −ta*

   face −Loc an iron plate −Acc lay

   (lit.) to lay an iron plate onto face

   (int.) 'Someone is brazen-faced, impudent.'

The *face* in the idioms in (60a −b) and (61a −h) represents a person's honor or reputation. We can say that the conceptual metaphor HONOR IS A FACE and the metonymy THE FACE FOR THE PERSON exist in the conceptual systems of the English and Korean speakers.

2) Idioms without Common Conceptual Metaphors between English and Korean

In this section, I will deal with idioms which do not share common conceptual metaphors between English and Korean. Korean *kho* 'nose', *kan* 'liver' and *kasum* 'breast or heart' will be discussed.

NOSE

While English *nose* refers to too much concern or interest, Korean *kho* 'nose' coherently represents a person's pride. Let us consider the following expressions.

(62) a. A troublesome woman with her nose into everything

b. Keep your nose out of my affairs!

(63) a. *khostay −ka nop −ta*

the bridge of the nose −Nom be.high

(lit.) Someone's nose bridge is high.

(int.) 'Someone is proud or someone is haughty.'

b. *khostay −ka sey −ta*

the bridge of the nose −Nom be.strong

(lit.) Someone's nose bridge is strong.

(int.) 'Someone is stubborn or someone is defiant.'

c. *khostay −lul kkekk −ta*

the bridge of the nose −Acc break

(lit.) to break someone's nose bridge

(int.) 'to humble someone's pride'

In Korean, if a person's nose is puffed up, then the meaning is 'to be proud or to be haughty'. In other words, pride is described by a body part, *kho*. The idioms are made and used based on the conceptual metaphor PRIDE IS A PERSON's NOSE, which is under the conceptual metaphor EMOTION IS A BODY PART. Other examples are suggested in (64).

(64) a. *kho −ka napcakhayci −ta*

nose −Nom become flat

(lit.) Someone's nose becomes flat.

(int.) 'Someone is humiliated.'

b. *kho −ka ppaci −ta*

nose−Nom come out

(lit.) Someone's nose comes out.

(int.) 'Someone is inactive and lifeless.'

Let us consider the following example in Korean.

(65) *kho kaps −ul ha −ta*

nose value−Acc do

(lit.) to do someone's nose value

(int.) 'to behave like a hero'

(65) is used to mean that a man behaves like a hero or with dignity, which is worth his pride. Some idioms including *kho* appear to be unrelated with pride, but they are also related with a person's pride. Such example is suggested in (66).

(66) *kho −ka ppittwuleci −key*

nose−Nom slantwise

(lit.) (to the degree that) someone's nose is slantwise

(int.) '(Someone is) so drunken (as not to feel shame).'

(66) is used when a person drinks alcohol so much that he cannot feel shame.

Kho is used to mention a part of a thing when it has the similar form to *kho* or it refers to the same part as a person's nose in the face. It is a kind of an "image" metaphor. The examples are shown in (67).

(67) a. *shinpal −kho*

   (lit.) shoe nose

   (int.) 'the toe of a shoe'

b. *pesen −kho*

   (lit.) Korean sock nose

   (int.) 'the toe of a Korean sock'

c. *kho −panul*

   (lit.) nose needle

   (int.) 'a crochet needle used in knitting'

(67c) has a hook and the hook is prominent like a person's nose. Metonymically *kho* means snivel which is in the nose. The examples are in (68).

(68) a. *kho −lul phwul −ta*

   nose −Acc discharge

   (lit.) Someone discharges his / her nose.

   (int.) 'Someone blows his / her nose.'

b. *kho −lul hulli −ta*

   nose −Acc shed

   (lit.) Someone sheds his / her nose.

   (int.) 'Someone runs at the nose.'

c. *kho −lul takk −ta*

   nose −Acc wipe

(lit.) to wipe one's nose

(int.) 'to wipe one's snivel'

Generally children have runny nose, so that *kho* itself does not have such meaning but some idioms including *kho* like (69) refer to children.

(69) a. *kho mut −un ton*

nose smearing money

(lit.) snivel smearing money

(int.) 'a child's pocket money'

b. *kho hullikay*

nose running kid

'a snotty-nosed kid, a sniveler'

LIVER

Liver is a very important part in our internal organs. Korean has several idioms including *kan* 'liver'. Unlike English *liver*, Korean *kan* represents a coherent concept of courage. Therefore, a person with a big liver is very courageous, while a person with a small liver is very cowardly. They are based on the conceptual metaphor EMOTION IS A BODY PART.

(70) a. *kan −i khu −ta*

liver−Nom be.big

(lit.) Someone's liver is big.

(int.) 'Someone is bold.'

b. *kan −i cak −ta*

liver−Nom be.small

(lit.) Someone's liver is small.

(int.) 'Someone is chicken-hearted.'

c. *kan −i khongal −man −hayci −ta*

liver−Nom bean−to the extent(Par)−become

(lit.) Someone's liver becomes the size of the bean.

(int.) 'Someone is frightened.'

d. *kan −i pwus −ta*

liver−Nom be.swollen

(lit.) Someone's liver is swollen.

(int.) 'Someone says or acts indiscreetly because of recklessness.'

(70d) is an impolite style of speech of (70a) *kan −i khu −ta*. The idioms are based on the conceptual metaphor COURAGE IS A LIVER which is under the conceptual metaphor EMOTION IS A BODY PART. Sometimes *kan* refers to heart, which is also related with courage.

(71) a. *kan −ul coli −ta,*

liver−Acc boil down

(lit.) to boil down liver

(int.) 'Someone worries oneself.'

b. *kan −i malu −ta*

liver−Nom dry up

(lit.) Someone's liver dries up.

    (int.) 'Someone worries oneself.'

c. *kan −i tha −ta*

liver−Nom burn

(lit.) Someone's liver burns.

(int.) 'Someone is anxious.'

d. *kancang −ul thaywu −ta*

liver−Acc make burn

(lit.) to make someone's liver burn

(int.) 'to make someone anxious'

e. *kan −ul noki −ta*

liver−Acc melt

(lit.) to melt someone's liver

(int.) 'to melt someone's heart'

f. *kan −ul ppay −cwu −ta*

liver−Acc take out and give

(lit.) to take out and give someone's liver

(int.) 'to flatter other persons'

(71e) has two meanings. One is to make a person very anxious, and the other is to charm others' hearts.

Some idioms including *kan* mean surprise or shock, and this is also related with courage or heart. Therefore, they are also based on the conceptual metaphor EMOTION IS A BODY PART. The examples are suggested in (72).

(72) a. *kan −i tteleci −ta*

liver−Nom be.detached

> (lit.) Someone's liver falls apart.
>
> (int.) 'Someone is much startled.'

b. *kan −i khongal −man −hayci −ta,*

  liver−Nom bean−to the extent(Par)−become

  (lit.) Someone's liver becomes the size of a bean.

  (int.) 'Someone is extremely terrified.'

c. *kan −i okulatul −ta*

  liver−Nom curl up

  (lit.) Someone's liver curls up.

  (int.) 'Someone is extremely terrified.'

In the following examples, *kan* does not represent courage but internal organs or heart.

(73) a. *kan −ey kipyel −to an ka −ta*

  liver−Loc notice−even(Par) not go

  (lit.) not to give any notice to the liver

  (int.) '(Food is so little that) it barely satisfy one's stomach.'

b. *kan −ey chaci −anh −ta*

  liver−Loc satisfy not

  (lit.) not to satisfy someone's liver

  (int.) 'not to satisfy someone'

As seen in the above, Korean *kan* 'liver' represents courage or heart, so that many expressions including it are also based on the conceptual metaphor EMOTION IS A BODY PART which contains the sub-stage conceptual metaphor COURAGE IS A LIVER.

HEART, BREAST

Korean *kasum* refers to the breast or the chest of the body. In Korean, it mainly stands for heart metonymically, so that people think *meli* 'head' stands for reason and *kasum* 'heart' means emotion. English *breast* also has both the physical meaning and the mental meaning, but the mental meaning (heart) is only one of the several meanings and *breast* usually refers to one part of the body. Rather, *bosom* is used to represent the mental meaning like tender feelings.

Kasum has a lot of idioms including it. Physically it refers to the breast or the chest of the body, and some idiom related with it is in (74).

    (74) *kasum −ul phye −ta*

        breast − Acc stretch

        (lit.) to stretch one's breast

        (int.) 'to stretch, to throw out one's chest'

Metonymically *kasum* also refers to the heart, the internal organ of the body, and the example is (75).

    (75) *kasum −i twukunkeli −ta*

        heart − Nom throb

        'Someone's heart throbs.'

Many idioms with *kasum* are associated with the meaning of mind or bosom.

(76) a. *kasum −ul yel −ta*

breast−Acc open

(lit.) to open one's breast

(int.) 'to open one's innermost feelings'

   b. *kasum −ul thele −noh −ta*

breast−Acc disclose

(lit.) to disclose one's breast

(int.) 'to open one's mind and tell frankly'

Kasum is also used to stand for the conscience which is considered to be there. It is a kind of metonymy THE PART FOR THE WHOLE.

(77) a. *kasum −ey son −ul enc −ta*

breast−Loc hand−Acc put

(lit.) to put one's hand on the breast

(int.) 'to think conscientiously'

   b. *kasum −i ttukkumha −ta*

breast−Nom be pricked

(lit.) Someone's breast is pricked.

(int.) 'to cut to the heart, to go home to the heart'

   c. *kasum −ey ccilli −ta*

breast−Loc be pricked

(lit.) Someone's breast is pricked.

(int.) 'to cut to the heart, to go home to the heart'

Kasum is used to represent deep emotion. This is based on the conceptual metaphor EMOTION IS A BODY PART. To speak specifically, the sub-stage conceptual metaphor FEELING IS A HEART, which is under the conceptual metaphor EMOTION IS A BODY PART, organizes and controls our language and thought.

(78) a. *kasum —ey wa —tah —ta*

   breast—Loc come and touch

   (lit.) to come to the breast and touch

   (int.) 'to make a deep emotion'

   b. *kasum —ul phako —tul —ta*

   breast—Acc permeate

   (lit.) to permeate the breast

   (int.) 'to make a deep emotion'

   c. *kasum —ul wulli —ta*

   breast—Acc move

   (lit.) to move the breast

   (int.) 'to give a deep emotion'

   d. *kasum —ul cekshi —ta*

   breast—Acc make wet

   (lit.) to make wet the breast

   (int.) 'to give a deep emotion'

   e. *kasum —i mungkhulha —ta*

   breast—Nom be choked with (grief or something)

   (lit.) Someone's breast is choked with something.

   (int.) 'to have a lump in one's throat'

(79) a. *kasum —i ttukep —ta*

breast—Nom be.hot

(lit.) Someone's breast is hot.

(int.) 'Someone is very passionate.'

b. *kasum —i nelp —ta*

breast—Nom be.wide

(lit.) Someone's breast is wide.

(int.) 'Someone is generous.'

c. *kasum —i ttattusha —ta*

breast—Nom be.warm

(lit.) Someone's breast is warm.

(int.) 'Someone is warm-hearted.'

d. *kasum —ulo nukki —ta*

breast—Inst feel

(lit.) to feel with breast

(int.) 'to feel with heart, to feel keenly'

In (78) *kasum* refers to emotion in a broad sense, and in (79) it represents passion or sentiment, the opposite of reason.

We mention *kasum* when we want to remember something, such as (80). In this case, *kasum* indicates mind in a broad sense. The meaning of the following examples is to remember something in someone's mind.

(80) a. *kasum —ey kancikha —ta*

breast—Loc keep

(lit.) to keep in the breast

(int.) 'to keep in heart'

124

b. *kasum —ey sayki —ta*

breast—Loc engrave

(lit.) to engrave in the breast

(int.) 'to engrave in heart'

c. *kasum —ey pakhi —ta*

breast—Loc get stuck

(lit.) to get stuck in the breast

(int.) 'to get stuck in heart'

Kasum is also used to represent surprise or broken heart.

(81) a. *kasum —i telkhengha —ta*

breast—Nom bang

(lit.) Someone's breast bangs.

(int.) 'Someone is greatly surprised'

b. *kasum —i naylye —anc —ta*

breast—Nom fall and sit down

(lit.) Someone's breast falls down.

(int.) 'Someone is greatly surprised.'

c. *kasum —ul alh —ta*

breast—Acc be.sick

(lit.) Someone is sick at the breast.

(int.) 'Someone has a chest trouble, someone has an agony in mind'

d. *kasum —i theci —ta*

breast—Nom get broken

(lit.) Someone's breast gets broken.

        (int.) 'Someone is heartbroken.'

  e. *kasum −i cciceci −ta*

    breast−Nom tear

    (lit.) Someone's breast tears.

    (int.) 'Someone is heartbroken.'

  f. *kasum −i taptapha −ta*

    breast−Nom be choked up

    (lit.) Someone's breast is choked up

    (int.) 'Someone feels choked up, someone feels frustrated.'

  g. *kasum −i hwulyenha −ta*

    breast−Nom feel relieved

    (lit.) Someone's breast feels relieved.

    (int.) 'Someone feels relieved.'

  h. *kasum −i thui −ta*

    breast−Nom get cleared

    (lit.) Someone's breast gets cleared.

    (int.) 'Someone feels free.'

(81c) means both the chest trouble in the body physically and trouble or agony in mind mentally. (81f) originally refers to the condition under which someone is hard to breathe, but it is often used to the frustrated situation. To represent the condition where difficulties are removed, we use (81g) or (81h).

To sum up, Korean *kasum* coherently refers to emotion or feelings because the conceptual metaphor FEELING IS A HEART underlies in our thought and *kasum* metonymically stands for heart.

CHAPTER 4

Significance of Learning Idioms in English Education

This chapter deals with idiom comprehension and pedagogical contribution of idiom studies based on some experiments on Korean students' understanding of English idioms. In particular, I will address to the following questions: (i) Are there some differences on idiom comprehension between native speakers and non-native speakers? (ii) Is the context helpful to non-native speakers in understanding English idioms? (iii) Does the transparency or opacity of metaphoricity of an idiom have an influence on the idiom comprehension? (iv) Is conceptual knowledge suggested by cognitive linguistics helpful to learn English idioms?

Section 4.1 surveys previous studies on idiom comprehension and I suggest that some distinctions be considered in idiom comprehension according to idiom types. Section 4.2 is about idiom comprehension of children and non-native speakers. Children and non-native speakers have common things in understanding idioms. Section 4.3 and 4.4 are about experiment and discussion on idiom comprehension of Korean speakers learning English.

1. Different Views on Comprehension of Idioms

In general, there are two opposite views of idiom comprehension. The first view argues that idioms are big words; the other argues that the meaning of each component word in an idiom contribute to the whole idiomatic meaning.

The former view is based on the claim that idioms are not compositional, so that the meaning of each word in an idiom does not contribute to the idiomatic meaning. Bobrow and Bell (1973) propose "the idiom list hypothesis", Swinney and Cutler (1979) suggest "the lexical representation hypothesis", and Gibbs (1980) proposes "the direct access hypothesis" or "the direct interpretation hypothesis". The latter view is that the component meaning plays an important role in the interpretation and use of idioms. Cacciari and Tabossi (1988) suggest "the configuration hypothesis", and Gibbs and Nayak (1989) suggest "the decompositionality hypothesis". In the following, I will examine these various theories one by one.

Bobrow and Bell (1973) assume that idioms are represented on the mental idiom list aside from the mental lexicon. When people encounter idioms, the literal meanings of words are firstly examined. If the literal meaning is not interpretable at that context, then the idiom list is examined. When the word string is in the list, the listed idiom meaning is the intended meaning. A crucial disadvantage of this approach is that idioms are always understood based on literal senses at first; thus, idiomatic senses of idioms always take a longer time to be understood than their literal senses.

Swinney and Cutler (1979) suggest "Lexical Representation Hypothesis", which claims that to understand an idiom is to simultaneously compute both its literal meaning and non-literal meaning. That is, the computation of figurative meaning and literal meaning begins from the first word of an idiom string. When we encounter an idiom, its literal and non-literal meanings are derived simultaneously, and if it matches with "a long word", i.e., an idiom, in the mental lexicon, the long-word idiom is also activated. Idiomatic meanings can be identified faster than literal phrase meanings because word recognition is usually faster than phrase comprehension. For example, *kick the bucket* is understood as 'die' rather than 'boot the pail.'

Their lexical representation hypothesis, however, is rejected by syntactic and lexical flexibility of some idioms. Many idioms do not behave like a word, but like an ordinary phrase. Some idioms undergo syntactic operations like passivization. If *pull one's leg* is simply a long word, one component *pull* in the string cannot be syntactically productive and passivization such as *one's leg is pulled* is impossible. In addition, some idioms retain their figurative meanings in spite of the change of a word in the idiom. For instance, *break the ice* and *crack the ice* have the same figurative meaning.

Gibbs (1980, 1985) proposes "a direct interpretation hypothesis," which argues that people directly understand the meaning of idioms without literal interpretation. He measured the time of understanding some expressions in their literal use and idiomatic use. Let us take one example, *You can let the cat out of the bag.* Its literal meaning is that you are allowed to let the cat from the sack, and the idiomatic meaning is that you can reveal the secret. The result shows that the subjects understood the idiomatic meaning faster than the literal meaning, which suggests that people understand the meaning of idioms without literal interpretation. But he proposes that idioms have differences in the degree of undergoing syntactic operations and in the degree of holding figurative interpretations. Therefore, he thinks the way idioms are represented and accessed is much more complex than the lexical representation hypothesis. In sum, the more conventional, familiar, and frozen an idiom is, the more people tend not to analyze its literal meaning. However, some idioms may have stronger lexical status than other idioms.

Gibbs and Gonzales (1985) investigate, through three experiments, the influence of syntactic frozenness on the comprehension and memory of idiomatic expressions through three experiments. The results show that the subjects processed idiomatic expressions faster than non-idiomatic control strings and that they processed frozen idioms faster than flexible idioms. In conclusion, idioms are part of normal lexicon, but they are accessed differently according to the degree of syntactic frozenness.

In Cacciari and Tabossi's (1988) configuration hypothesis, idioms are regarded as familiar and memorized strings of words. When people encounter such a string, word meanings are activated and at the same time the string itself is recognized as a unit or a configuration. The prototypical configurations are lines of poetry or snatches of songs. If we hear first some words of the poetry or the song, we automatically remember the rest part of the string. Therefore, the individual word meaning of the configuration may or may not contribute the whole meaning of the idiom, but it plays a part within the idiom. According to Cacciari and Tabossi (1988), idioms are not non-decomposable units but familiar word sequences. The interpretation of idioms is context-dependent, and idioms differ in the degree that the component word meaning contributes to the whole sequence meaning.

Similarly, Gibbs and Nayak's (1989) decompositionality hypothesis proposes that idioms differ from each other in the degree of semantic analyzability. Syntactic and lexical flexibility is something to do with semantic analyzability.

Idiom use and idiom comprehension are important part of everyday speech. Fluent speakers can use not only the language itself but also the language within the culture. Therefore, idioms must be recognized and identified not only as their own meaning but also as linguistic entities. The role of word meaning is found in slips of the tongue. Even if a speaker uses *swallow the bullet* instead of *bite the bullet* ('to face something unpleasant with courage'), the hearer understands the intended meaning and sometimes both the speaker and the hearer even do not notice the error. Therefore, in everyday speech, people usually depend on familiar and memorized chunks of speech, whose meanings come from everyday experience such as titles of books, movies, and songs.

Glucksberg (1993) proposes that idioms are not unanalyzable wholes but linguistic and conceptual entities. Hearers understand speakers' intention at the discourse context, uniting literal, stipulated —idiomatic, and allusional meanings of idioms. And the choice of words and idioms is determined by the relation among component elements. For example, *kick the bucket* is used when death is unanticipated or abrupt. The concept of quick death is represented in the action of kicking.

In conclusion, idiom comprehension has various processes according to the idiom types. The first distinction we should consider is compositional idioms vs. non-compositional idioms. A compositional idiom is understood with the composition of the meaning of each word in the idiom, while a non-compositional idiom is identified as a long word. The second is conventional idioms vs. novel idioms. Conventional idioms are frozen idioms, so that people within the culture use them easily and frequently. Novel idioms are based on semantic properties that provide some kind of resemblance. From the standpoint of non-native speakers, conventional idioms are difficult to understand unless they know the convention. In the case of novel idioms, non-native speakers also have difficulty in comprehending them partly because most of them include metaphor. The third is idioms of concrete actions vs. idioms of abstract and complex cognitions. The idioms representing concrete actions are easier to be understood than the idioms of abstract and complex cognitions.

2. Children's Understanding of Idioms

Figurative schemes such as metaphor, metonymy, irony and idioms play an important role in everyday thoughts and language because they organize our experience. The reason people use various figurative schemes is that various processes of figuration shape human cognition. Therefore, in understanding metaphors and metonymies, conceptual and pragmatic knowledge is required.

According to the experiment of Gibbs and Gonzales (1985), adults process syntactically frozen idioms faster than syntactically flexible idioms because the former are lexicalized in the mental lexicon and are accessed directly. Children also understand syntactically frozen idioms better than syntactically flexible idioms. The former are used in fewer syntactic forms than the latter. Like adults, children also understand metaphorically transparent idioms more easily than metaphorically opaque idioms.

According to Gardner (1974), children can map meanings of words and phrases from one domain to another domain. In other words, children can make metaphorical mappings between source and target domain.

Children have difficulty in explaining the figurative meanings of idioms without supporting context. Like the second language learners, children who are English native speakers interpret idioms literally if the context is not given. Especially, children from the age of 5 to 9 do not completely recognize the relation between idiomatic phrases and their figurative meanings. Therefore, context leads them to understand figurative interpretation. But adults tend to give figurative interpretation to idiomatic phrases even in strong literal contexts (Gibbs 1980, 1986).

According to Gibbs (1987), no single model can explain how children learn the meanings of idioms. Idioms do not form a homogeneous class in the way people acquire and remember them. Metaphorically transparent idioms may be acquired by metaphorically reasoning strategies because the figurative meanings of the idioms are transparently related to the meanings of individual parts, while metaphorically opaque idioms may be learned in more of a rote manner. This strategy may be particularly useful in learning the meanings of idioms that are not literally well-formed such as *by and large*. Gibbs (1987) presents both kinds of strategies might be required to learn the meanings of idioms with multiple interpretations. For example, when *give a hand* means 'to help out,' a metaphorically reasoning strategy is used because it has a metaphorically transparent meaning, whereas when it means 'to applaud,' a rote strategy is required to acquire the more opaque interpretation.

Levorato (1993) claims that children's acquisition of idioms is not a simple matter of learning only conventional expressions passively but a process including complex linguistic and cognitive skills. His suggestion is that to make and understand idiomatic expressions has something to do with the progress of figurative language, so that it is important to develop figurative competence. Figurative competence is increased with the development of whole series of linguistic skills.

Second language learners may be similar to children in idiom comprehension process. But non-native speakers tend to analyse the individual meaning of idiom component regardless of idiom types like the claim of Bobrow and Bell (1973). After they learn the meaning of an idiom, they may process the idiomatic meaning first, while they may analyse the individual meaning in the case of idioms they don't know. Therefore, the relation between the components of idioms and their meaning must be considered because they always analyse the component meaning until the idiomatic expression is recognized as one configuration. In other words, non-native speakers easily understand the idioms with transparent relations between the idiom components and their meanings such as *break the ice*, whereas they may not guess the meaning of the idioms with opaque relations such as *cook one's goose*.

break the ice	*cook one's goose*
(to ease the nervousness or formality in a social situation)	(to ruin a person's chances of success)
break – – – – – – – – –> ease ice – – – – – – – – –> social tension	cook – – – – – – – –> ? ruin goose – – – – – – –> ? chances

In order to improve figurative competence foreign language learners need to increase communicative competence. In other words, they should develop communicative abilities as well as linguistic skills. Native speakers have communicative abilities which are made up of linguistic skills and pragmatic skills. But foreign students learning English usually make a focus on linguistic skills, which are about verbal elements of vocabulary, phonology, syntax, and so on.

Communicative abilities mean the appropriate use of language plus nonverbal elements. Nonverbal elements are acquired with culture, customs, and social situations. Therefore, it is necessary to consider culture, convention, and way of thinking which are reflected on verbal elements. Especially, idioms have something to do with culture or convention, so that in many cases English and Korean idioms do not correspond. For example, in Korean, "Her hand is big" does not mean 'The size of her hand is big' but it means 'She prepares much more food than what she needs (sometimes extravagantly),' in Korean "Her hand is pungent" means 'She has an evil hand', and "His nose became flat" means 'He was humiliated'.

In order to develop a figurative competence, foreign students should note metaphors and metonymies. Metaphors make students understand from the well-known to the less well-known in a vivid and memorable way, and therefore they help students to learn. In other words, metaphors can provide a rational bridge from a given context of understanding (source) to a changed context of understanding (target).

Through this study of idioms and metaphors, I want to help non-native speakers of English to learn English idioms better by showing the similarities and differences of the conceptual metaphors that English and Korean idioms have.

3. Experiment

An experiment on English idioms was made with some native speakers of Korean who are learning English as a foreign language. Korean students were divided into two groups—an experiment group and a control group. Basic conceptual metaphors were explained to the experiment group, but not to the control group. They were selected randomly and their abilities and test marks on English were various.

The experiment was done in order to explore the following issues. First, does the explanation about conceptual metaphors involved in English idioms help the students to understand English idioms better? Second, when idioms are divided into three groups according to the relation between constituent meaning of an idiom and overall meaning of an idiom—transparent idioms, less transparent idioms, and opaque idioms, do non-native speakers show differences in understanding them like native speakers? Third, how much influence does the context make on the comprehension of idiom meaning? Fourth, how many different degrees of relation are there between the constituent meaning and the overall meaning according to the above idiom types?

The experiment was based on a questionnaire which was composed of three parts. The first part is about the difference the subjects show with regard to the idiom types (transparent, less transparent, and opaque idioms). The subjects were given nine English idioms: three belong to transparent idioms, three belong to less transparent idioms, and three belong to opaque idioms. The transparent idioms include *break the ice, bite off more than one can chew,* and *on pins and needles.* The less transparent idioms contain *give up the ship, carry coals to New Castle,* and *beat around the bush.* The opaque idioms are *cook one's goose, pull a fast one,* and *face the music.* The idioms were classified based on Glucksberg (1993) and Gibbs (1993).

The idioms were used with some context. Each idiom has six questions. The first question is what the meaning of the idiom is, and the second question is to ask the subjects to choose the meaning of the idiom out of the four illustrative examples. The students were asked to answer the questions in the order of the questions so as not to get some hints from the illustrative examples of the next questions, but most of them might take some suggestions from the illustrative examples. Therefore, they made a good guess about the meaning of the idiom in the second question although most of them answered that they didn't know the meaning in the first question at all. The third question is about the degree of their knowing the idiom. The fourth question is about the role of the context in the case that they didn't know the meaning of the idiom at all. The fifth question is about the degree of the role of the context in the case of each idiom. The sixth question is about the degree of the role of the constituent meaning. In other words, how much does each constituent meaning help them understand the overall meaning of the idiom? A sample of the questionnaire is given below.[22] The example

---

22) ① The questions were written down in Korean in order for the subjects not to misunderstand the meanings of the questions, and the sample is translated into English.

is on the next page.

The next part of the experiment is about the role of the conceptual metaphors in the recognition and the categorization of some idioms. After showing some examples with a specific explanation about the conceptual metaphors, the subjects were asked to divide the given idioms into two groups according to their meanings. Most of the subjects didn't know the exact meanings of the idioms suggested in the questionnaire, but model examples may help them. They were also asked to make a title of each group of the idioms and to make an explanation about each idiom. The experiment group of the subjects (25 persons) were once given some explanation about the conceptual metaphors, while the control group (22 persons) did not get any such explanation.

---

② The original questionnaire is provided in the Appendix.

bite off more than one can chew

Roger always sign up for the hardest courses on campus. On hiking trips, he always chooses the most dangerous trails even though he doesn't have enough hiking experience. He is the sort of person who always **bites off more than he can chew.**

(1) What do you think the meaning of the idiom "bite off more than one can chew" is?

(2) What action corresponds to biting off more than he can chew?
   a) Chewing something that is bitten.
   b) Doing something that is beyond his abilities.
   c) Biting something that is too much.
   d) Attacking someone who is too rude or too arrogant

(3) Are you ignorant of the idiom originally?

1	2	3	4
not know at all	know little	know a little	know completely

(4) Do you come to guess its meaning due to the context given with the idiom though you don't know it originally?

yes	no

(5) In the case of this question, how much help do you think the context gives in understanding the meaning of the idiom?

1	2	3	4
not help at all	help little	help a little	help very much

(6) In the case of this question, how much help do you think the meaning of the individual word in the idiom gives in understanding the composite meaning of the idiom?

1	2	3	4
not help at all	help little	help a little	help very much

The third part is about the idioms with color terms. Regarding the six color terms *black, white, red, blue, green* and *yellow*, the subjects were asked about each color term idiom—about the meaning and the degree of their awareness. Among the color term idioms, there are some invented idioms based on Korean color term idioms in order to compare their understanding between ordinary English idioms and the invented idioms. The final question of the third part is about the associated concepts of each color. This is added in order to ensure the native speaker's intuition about some Korean color terms.

4. Discussion

As for the three types of idioms, the subjects show a distinction of comprehension as expected. Both the experiment group and the control group understood the transparent idioms better than the opaque idioms. The experiment group did a little better than the control group, but the difference is not significant enough. This question is not for the comparison of the two groups but for the comparison of three idiom types. So, the results were computed by integrating the experiment and the control groups.

In the case of the transparent idioms, more than half of the students answered the meanings correctly and 88% chose the correct meanings out of the illustrative examples. The contributing degree of the context to help find out the idiom meaning is 3.3. That is, the context makes much contribution to finding out the meaning of idioms. The degree is divided into 4 categories. Category 1 is that the context does not help find out the meaning of the idiom at all, category 2 means that it hardly helps, category 3 means that the context helps to some extent, and category 4 means that the context helps very much. By contrast, the contributing degree of the constituent meaning to the overall meaning of the idioms is 2.86. This suggests that the context contributes more to figuring out the overall meaning of idioms than the constituent meaning.

As for the less transparent idioms, 43% answered the meanings correctly, and 66% chose the correct answer among the illustrative examples. The contributing degree of the context is 3.21 and the contributing degree of the constituent meaning is 2.67.

In the case of the opaque idioms, only less than 10% answered the meanings correctly, while 41% chose the correct answer out of the illustrative examples. The contributing degree of the context is 2.87 and the contributing degree of the constituent meaning is 2.17.

The subjects did not know most of the idioms, so the degree that they didn't know the idioms at all is similar in the three types of idioms: transparent idioms 1.27; less transparent idioms 1.47; opaque idioms 1.21. Moreover, the degree of taking hints from the context is not much distinctive among the three types of idioms. That is to say, the subjects take hints about the idiom meaning from the context regardless of idiom types. Therefore, the context makes considerable influence on the comprehension of idioms. But the constituent meaning does not contribute to the overall meaning of idioms in the case of opaque idioms (2.17). This supports what is generally believed, that is, the meaning of the individual word is not related with the overall meaning of the idiom in the case of opaque idioms.

The results of the first part of the experiment are all represented in Table 7 and graphically represented in Charts 1 and 2 below.

Table 7. Comprehension of Idioms according to Their Types

types of idioms	degree of correct answering	degree of correct answering among examples	degree of understanding (1: not know, -4: know completely)	degree of feeling that context is helpful	contributing degree of context (1 -4)	contributing degree of constituent meaning (1 -4)
transparent idioms	0.54334	0.88334	1.266068	0.84394	3.297046	2.855126
less transparent idioms	0.431212	0.663939	1.466364	0.839379	3.213636	2.672424
opaque idioms	0.099394	0.414848	1.205152	0.715151	2.868182	2.17394

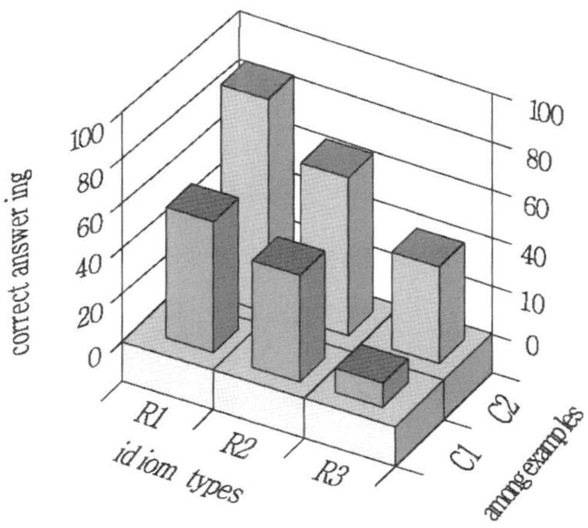

Chart 1. Degree of Correct answering according to the Idiom Types

The front bars represent the degrees of the correct answering according to the idiom types, and the rear bars represent the degrees of the correct answering among illustrative examples. Chart 1 represents that the more transparent an idiom is, the better the subjects guessed the right meaning. The difference between the front and the rear bars means that the subjects guessed the idiom meaning easily among illustrative examples.

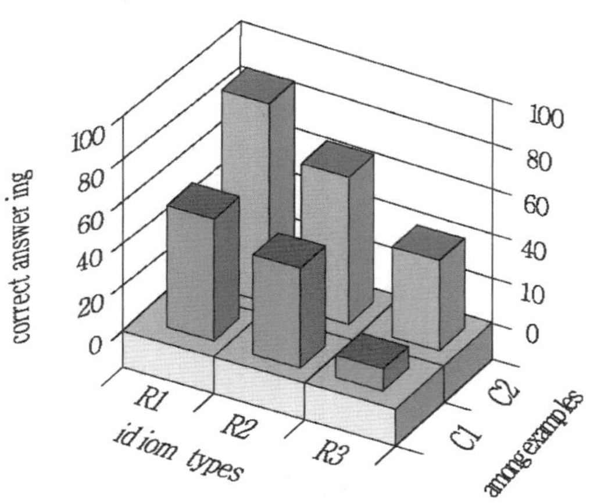

Chart 2. Degree of Contribution of the
Context and the Constituent meaning

The front bars represent the contributing degrees of the context according to the three idiom types, and the rear bars represent the contributing degrees of the constituent meaning to the overall meaning of idioms. Chart 2 means that the context rather than the individual word meaning more contributes to understanding the overall idiom meaning. Therefore, the contributing degree of the context is relatively higher than that of the component word meaning regardless of the idiom types.

As for the role of the conceptual metaphors in the students' understanding of some idioms, the experiment group categorized the given idioms better than the control group. They were taught the conceptual metaphors idioms may contain. The result was that the experiment group showed a higher rate of knowledge in the categorization of given idioms. In other words, the experiment group categorized better than the control group in making two groups with the given idioms and in giving the titles to the categorized groups respectively. In order to compare the averages between the experiment group and the control group, the "t−test" was used, which is useful when the size of the sample is small. The average, the standard deviation, and the number of each group are presented in Table 8.[23]

Table 8. The average and standard deviation of each group (level of significance .05)

group	average	standard deviation	number of sample	degree of freedom $(N-1)$
experiment group	$\overline{X_e}=3.88$	$S_e=1.2335584$	$N_e=25$	$df=24$
control group	$\overline{X_c}=2.818182$	$S_c=1.9901323$	$N_c=22$	$df=21$

$\overline{X_e}$: The average of the experiment group

$\overline{X_c}$: The average of the control group

S_e : The standard deviation of the experiment group

S_c : The standard deviation of the control group

---

23) The average and the standard deviation of each idiom are added in the Appendix.

146

N_e : The number of the experiment group

N_c : The number of the control group

df : The degree of freedom which is a number that can have any value freely with keeping average.

To explain the degree of freedom more specifically, in the data where the size of the sample is four, and their values are 2. 3. 5. and 2 respectively, the degree of freedom is 3. In the sample of four persons, three persons can have any value freely but the rest one person must have a fixed value in order that the sum of deviations may be zero. So, the degree of freedom is 3.

$$t-\text{value} = \frac{\overline{X_e} - \overline{X_c}}{S(\overline{X_e} - \overline{X_c})} = \frac{\overline{X_e} - \overline{X_c}}{\sqrt{\left(\frac{S_e}{\sqrt{N_e}}\right)^2} + \sqrt{\left(\frac{S_c}{\sqrt{N_c}}\right)^2}} = 2.16$$

In order to reject the null hypothesis,[24] the $t-$value between the two groups must be high enough to ensure that the difference is not accidental. The total df of the two groups is $Ne-1+Nc-1=45$, and it is between 40 and 60 in the figure of Critical values of t. The cell intersected by $df=40$ and by the level of significance (.05) is 2.021. And the cell intersected by $df=60$ and by the level of significance is 2.000. In other words, the $t-$critical value is between 2.021 and 2.000, while the $t-$value that was computed in the experiment (2.16) is higher than the former (between 2.021 and

---

24) The null hypothesis is that the sample group is not different from the population. Two sample groups are chosen from the same population.

2.000). It can thus be said that the difference is significant statistically. Therefore, we can claim that a prior explanation of conceptual metaphors is effective in the comprehension and categorization of idioms.

In the survey on the concepts the color terms evoke, it was proved that the subjects had the associated concepts based on the conceptual metaphors I suggested in section 3.2. Let us take some examples. With regard to the associated concepts the color terms *black* and *white* have, over 90% of the subjects answered the concepts based on the conceptual metaphor QUALITY IS A COLOR. In other words, the conceptual metaphors BADNESS IS BLACK and GOODNESS IS WHITE prevail in their concepts. The color terms *red, blue, green* and *yellow* have more various concepts. Nevertheless, the subjects showed that their thought were influenced by the conceptual metaphors TEMPERATURE IS A COLOR including HOTNESS IS RED and COLDNESS IS BLUE, EMOTION IS A COLOR including ANGER IS RED and MELANCHOLY IS BLUE, and SIGNAL IS A COLOR containing DANGER IS RED and SAFETY OR PERMISSION IS GREEN. Table 9 shows the subjects' conception associated with color terms.

The associated conceptions of the color terms in Table 9 are generally corresponded with the answers the subjects gave to the color term idioms. As for the idioms with *black*, most subjects indicate that *black* has a negative image such as badness, malice, and unlawfulness. For example, the expressions *a black look* or *look black* mean 'an angry look' or 'look angry' respectively, but no subject did not guess so. Instead, most subjects thought that such phrases mean 'malignant look' or 'look malignant'. In contrast to *black*, the color term *red* represents anger. More than 26% of the subjects answered that the expressions *turn red* or *red heat* mean anger. That is to say, their conceptions are involved in the conceptual metaphors BADNESS IS BLACK and ANGER IS RED.

Table 9. The colors, the Associated Concepts and the Numbers mentioned

	black	white	red	blue
numbers mentioned	104	103	90	57
associated concepts	bad-related concepts 95	good-related concepts 93	hotness 34 danger 20 anger 10 blood 8 lasciviousness 4 others 14	coldness 23 melancholy 12 cleanness 11 others 11

	green	yellow	phuluta (green + blue)	
numbers mentioned	43	37	36	
associated concepts	safety 13 environment 11 freshness 5 peace 4 others 10	warmness 13 warning 6 brightness 4 others 14	refreshment 11 cleanness 10 hope 4 others 11	

More than 90% of the subjects answered that the color term *white* would have a good image. About 65% of the subjects made a right guess on the expression *a white flag*, perhaps because it has the same meaning as Korean *payk −ki* 'a white flag'. In other words, Korean speakers understand better when an English expression is used in the same way as in the Korean.

Let us consider some more color term idioms which the subjects tried to interpret English idioms with Korean conception. For example, the idiom *a red tape* stands for officialism or bureaucratism, but most of the subjects considered it as a pornographic video tape because *ppalkang* 'red' is sometimes used as a lascivious meaning in Korean. In the case of the idiom *blue blood*, about 30% of the subjects answered it would mean a cold-hearted person. The clue of such a guess they suggested was that *blue* represents coldness. That is, their thoughts are based on the conceptual metaphor COLDNESS IS BLUE under the conceptual metaphor TEMPERATURE IS A COLOR. The idiom *green-eyed* means an eye with envy. But no subject made a right guess. Rather, some subjects answered that they didn't know the meaning but it would have a positive meaning because the color term *green* had positive and favorable images such as environment and safety. No subject guessed the meaning of the phrase *too yellow to fight* in which yellow means 'cowardly'. In Korean *yellow* does not mean cowardice.

As for the invented idioms based on Korean, most students thought of *red lie* and *Someone's future is yellow* in the same way as Korean, *sayppalkan kecismal* '(vivid) red lie', *ssakswu −ka nolah −ta* 'someone's future is yellow'. Especially, in the case of the latter, some of the subjects referred to the Korean proverb *ttekip −i nolah −ta* 'sprout is yellow'. The two expressions show that we understand people in terms of plants. The yellow color of the leaves means showing no promise of success in human beings. That is, the conceptual metaphor PEOPLE ARE PLANTS prevails in our language and thought.

The invented idioms the subjects did not answer in the same way as Korean are *a white dress, a white remark* and *a yellow person*. A half of the subjects thought of *a white dress* as a wedding dress. The original purpose of my inventing the phrase is that it means Korean mourning clothes. But nowadays Korean people wear black clothes as well as white clothes as mourning clothes. Besides, *dress* usually refers to women's clothes. It seems that the expression *white clothes* may be suitable instead of *a white dress*.

A white remark was invented to mean Korean *huyn soli* 'white talk, white remark' which means a snobbish remark or a loud boast. No subject guessed rightly. Rather, some subjects thought of the expression as 'a true remark'. The reason may be that the conceptual metaphor GOODNESS IS WHITE exists in their conceptions.

The invented idiom *a yellow person* was intended to mean Korean *nolang —i* 'a stingy person'. Most of the subjects guessed it as a patient who does not have a good health. Maybe many subjects did not relate *nolang —i* with the color term *yellow*, and their thoughts are involved in the conceptual metaphor PEOPLE ARE PLANTS by which they understand people in terms of plants.

From the experiment, I conclude that people understand the meaning of words or phrases based on the conceptual metaphors. Therefore, the explanation about the basic conceptual metaphors in English may help Korean students with learning and understanding English idioms. In case English and Korean have similar conceptual metaphors or metonymies, we can use them in teaching English idioms. If English and Korean have different conceptual systems, we can teach English idioms effectively by way of teaching the conceptual systems and metaphors in advance.

CHAPTER 5

Conclusion

This study aims to show that many idioms are motivated in a certain system and they can be explained in a generalized way through the cognitive-linguistic study on idioms and metaphors, and therewith to contribute to English education in Korea by helping Korean speakers to understand and learn English idioms.

While the generative grammar assumes that idioms are of the same kind, they, in fact, constitute a continuum in their idiomaticity. That is, idioms are different in their compositionality, conventionality, and transparency. In Chapter 1, I examined the definitions of idioms proposed by many linguists.

Chapter 2 deals with some aspects of cognitive linguistics. I reviewed the prototype theory and examined the types of idioms based on the prototype theory. Idioms are often motivated by some conceptual metaphors and / or metonymies. I examined theories and

152

properties of metaphors and metonymies.

In Chapter 3, I showed that some conceptual metaphors independently existing in our conceptual system motivate many idioms including color terms and body-part terms. Section 3.1 deals with idioms including six basic color terms such as *black, white, red, green, yellow* and *blue*. The conceptual metaphors involved in the color terms are PEOPLE ARE PLANTS; QUALITY IS A COLOR which includes the sub-conceptual metaphors like BADNESS IS BLACK and GOODNESS IS WHITE; SIGNAL IS A COLOR containing DANGER IS RED and PERMISSION OR SAFETY IS GREEN; TEMPERATURE IS A COLOR including HOTNESS IS RED and COLDNESS IS BLUE; and EMOTION IS A COLOR like ANGER IS RED, ENVY IS GREEN and MELANCHOLY IS BLUE. Section 3.2 is a study of body-part term idioms with or without common conceptual metaphors and metonymies between English and Korean. English *head* and Korean *meli* or *kokay* 'head' are motivated by the conceptual metaphor HAVING CONTROL OR FORCE IS UP. A lot of idioms including English *hand* and Korean *son* 'hand' are based on the metonymy THE PART FOR THE WHOLE. Some idioms with English *face* and Korean *nach* or *elkwul* 'face' are on the basis of the metonymy THE FACE FOR THE PERSON, and other idioms are motivated by the conceptual metaphor HONOR IS A FACE. Most idioms including Korean *kho* 'nose', *kan* 'liver' and *kasum* 'breast, heart' coherently mean someone's pride, courage and feeling respectively. Therefore, they are based on the conceptual metaphor EMOTION IS A BODY PART which includes the sub-stage conceptual metaphors PRIDE IS A NOSE, COURAGE IS A LIVER and FEELING IS A HEART.

Chapter 4 deals with idiom comprehension theories and the experiments on the comprehension of English idioms by Korean speakers. The result of the experiment shows that idiom comprehension is influenced by context, idiom types, and the conceptual metaphors on which the idioms are based. The associated concepts the subjects have on the color terms in the experiment confirm the existence of conceptual metaphors I suggested in section 3.1.

Metaphors and metonymies are part of our everyday lives as well as part of our language; thus, studies on them merit further investigation. This thesis has dealt only with a small portion of idioms, but this type of research on idioms will help Koreans learning English to understand and use English idioms properly.

BIBLIOGRAPHY

Berlin, Brent and Paul Kay. 1969. *Basic Color Terms: Their Universality and Evolution*. Berkeley: University of California Press.

Bobrow, S. and S. Bell. 1973. On Catching on to Idiomatic Expressions. *Memory & Cognition* 1: 343−46.

Brown, R. 1958. *Words and Things*. New York: The Free Press.

Bybee, Joan L. 1985. *Morphology: A Study of the Relation between Meaning and Form*. Amsterdam: John Benjamins.

Bybee, Joan L. and Carol Lynn Moder. 1983. Morphological Classes as Natural Categories. *Language* 59: 251−70.

Cacciari, Cristina. 1993. The Place of Idioms in a Literal Metaphorical World. *Idioms: Processing, Structure, and Interpretation*, ed. by Cristina Cacciari and Patrizia Tabossi, 27−56. New Jersey: Lawrence Erlbaum Associates.

Cacciari, Cristina, and Patrizia Tabossi. 1988. The Comprehension of Idioms. *Journal of Memory and Language* 27: 668−83.

Cacciari, Cristina, and Sam Gluckberg. 1991. Understanding Idiomatic Expressions: The Contribution of Word Meanings. *Understanding Word and Sentence*, ed. by G. B. Simpson, 217−40. Amsterdam: Elsevier.

Chafe, Wallace L. 1968. Idiomaticity as an Anomaly in the Chomskyan Paradigm. *Foundations of Language* 4.2: 109−27.

Chafe, Wallace L. 1970. *Meaning and the Structure of Language*. Chicago: University of Chicago Press.

Chomsky, Noam. 1965. *Aspects of the Theory of Syntax*. Massachusetts: The M.I.T. Press.

Chomsky, Noam and Morris Halle. 1968. *The Sound Pattern of English*. New York and London: Harper & Row.

Cronk, Brian C., Susan D. Lima, and Wendy A. Schweigert. 1993. Idioms in Sentences: Effects of Frequency, Literalness, and Familiarity. *Journal of Psycholinguistic Research* 22.1: 59−81.

Cutler, Anne. 1982. Idioms: The Colder the Older. *Linguistic Inquiry* 13.2: 317−20.

Fauconnier, Gilles and Mark Turner. 1998. Principles of Conceptual Integration. *Discourse and Cognition: Bridging the Gap*, ed. by Jean−Pierre Koenig, 269−83. Stanford, California: CSLI Publications.

Fillmore, Charles J., Paul Kay, and Mary C. O'Connor. 1988. Regularity and Idiomaticity in Grammatical Constructions: The Case of *Let Alone*. *Language* 64: 501−38.

Fong, Heatherbell Nancy. 1988. *The Stony Idiom of the Brain: A Study in the Semantics and Syntax of Metaphors*. Ann Arbor: UMI Dissertation Services.

Forrester, Michael A. 1995. Tropic Implicature and Context in the Comprehension of Idiomatic Phrases. *Journal of Psycholinguistic Research* 24.1: 1−22.

Fraser, Bruce. 1970. Idioms within a Transformational Grammar. *Foundations of Language* 6.1: 22−42.

Fromkin, Victoria, and Robert Rodman. 1993. *An Introduction to Language*. (5th ed.) Harcourt Brace College Publishers.

Gardner, H. 1974. Metaphors and Modalities: how children project polar adjectives onto diverse domains. *Child Development* 45: 84−91.

Gibbs, Raymond W. Jr. 1980. Spilling the beans on Understanding and Memory for idioms in Conversation. *Memory and Cognition* 8: 449−56.

Gibbs, Raymond W. Jr. 1984. Literal Meaning and Psychological Theory. *Cognitive Psychology* 8: 191−219.

Gibbs, Raymond W. Jr. 1985. On the Process of Understanding Idioms.

Journal of Psycholinguistic Research 14.5: 465−72.

Gibbs, Raymond W. Jr. 1986. Skating on Thin Ice: literal meaning and understanding idioms in conversation. *Discourse Processes* 9: 17−30.

Gibbs, Raymond W. Jr. 1987. Linguistic Factors in Children's Understanding of Idioms. *Journal of Child Language* 14: 569−86.

Gibbs, Raymond W. Jr. 1993. Why Idioms Are Not Dead Metaphors. *Idioms: Processing, Structure, and Interpretation*, ed. by Cristina Cacciari and Patrizia Tabossi, 57−77. New Jersey: Lawrence Erlbaum Associates.

Gibbs, Raymond W. Jr. and Gayle P. Gonzales. 1985. Syntactic Frozenness in Processing and Remembering Idioms. *Cognition* 20: 243−59.

Gibbs, Raymond W. Jr. and Nandini P. Nayak. 1989. Psycholinguistic Studies on the Syntactic Behavior of Idioms. *Cognitive Psychology* 21: 100−38.

Gibbs, Raymond W. Jr. & Jennifer E. O'Brien. 1990. Idioms and Mental Imagery: The metaphorical motivation for idiomatic meaning. *Cognition* 36: 35−68.

Glucksberg, Sam. 1993. Idiom Meanings and Allusional Content. *Idioms: Processing, Structure, and Interpretation*, ed. by Cristina Cacciari and Patrizia Tabossi, 1−26. New Jersey: Lawrence Erlbaum Associates.

Grice, H. Paul. 1975. Logic and Conversation. *Syntax and Semantics* 3. ed. by Peter Cole and Jerry L. Morgan. New York: Academic Press.

Hankulhakhhoy. 1991. *Wulimal Khunsacen* [Korean Dictionary]. Seoul: Emunkak. (In Korean.)

Heine, Bernd. 1997. *Cognitive Foundations of Grammar*. New York and Oxford: Oxford University Press.

Heine, Bernd, Ulrike Claudi, and Friederike Hünnemeyer. 1991a. From Cognition to Grammar: Evidence from African Languages. *Approaches to Grammaticalization* Vol.1, ed. by Elizabeth C. Traugott and Bernd Heine, 149−87. Amsterdam: John Benjamins.

Heine, Bernd, Ulrike Claudi, and Friederike Hünnemeyer. 1991b. *Grammaticalization: A Conceptual Framework*. Chicago and London: The University of Chicago Press.

Hubbell, James A. and Michael W. O'Boyle. 1995. The Effects of Metaphorical and Literal Comprehension Processes on Lexical Decision Latency of Sentence Components. *Journal of Psycholinguistic Research* 24.4: 269−87.

Janus, Raizi A. and Thomas G. Bever. 1985. Processing of Metaphoric Language: An Investigation of the Three−Stage Model of Metaphor Comprehension. *Journal of Psycholinguistic Research* 14.5: 473−87.

Kim, Hyung−Sook. 1984. *A Study of English Idioms*. M. A. dissertation. Hankuk University of Foreign Studies.

Kim, Yunkyeng. 1996. *Ungyongenehak −kwa Thongkyeyhak*. [Applied Linguistics and Statistics] Seoul: Hankwukmunhwasa. (In Korean.)

Labov, William. 1973. The Boundaries of Words and their meanings. *New Ways of Analyzing Variation in English*. ed. by Bailey, C. N., and R. W. Shuy. Oxford: Oxford University Press.

Lakoff, George. 1972. Hedges: A Study in Meaning Criteria and the Logic of Fuzzy Concepts. *CLS* 8: 183−228.

Lakoff, George. 1977. Linguistic Gestalts. *CLS* 13: 236−87.

Lakoff, George. 1982. Categories: An Essay in Cognitive Linguistics. *Linguistics in the Morning Calm*, ed. by the Linguistic Society of Korea, 139−93. Seoul: Hanshin.

Lakoff, George. 1987. *Women, Fire, and Dangerous Things*. Chicago: The University of Chicago Press.

Lakoff, George. 1993. The Contemporary Theory of Metaphor. *Metaphor and Thought* (2nd edition), ed. by Andrew Ortony, 202−51. Cambridge: Cambridge University Press.

Lakoff, George and Mark Johnson. 1980. *Metaphors We Live By*. Chicago: The University of Chicago Press.

Langacker, Ronald W. 1987. *Foundations of Cognitive Grammar, Vol.1: Theoretical foundations*. Stanford, CA: Stanford University Press.

Langacker, Ronald W. 1991. *Concept, Image, and Symbol: The Cognitive Basis of Grammar*. Berlin and New York: Mouton de Gruyter.

Lee, Jongyeol. 2000. The Aspects of the Conceptual Integration through Metaphoric inferences. *Proceedings of the 6th Conference of the Discourse and Cognitive Linguistics Society of Korea*, 11–15. (In Korean.)

Lee, Keedong. 1997. Idiom, Metaphor, and Metonymy. *Discourse and Cognition* 4.1: 61–87. Seoul: Hankwukmunhwasa.

Lee, Unceng. 1994. *Kwukehak · Enehak Yonge Sacen* [A Terminology Dictionary of Korean Linguistics and Linguistics]. Seoul: Kwukemunhwasa. (In Korean.)

Levorato, M. Chiara. 1993. The Acquisition of Idioms and the Development of Figurative Competence. *Idioms: Processing, Structure, and Interpretation.* ed. by Cristina Cacciari and Patrizia Tabossi, 101–28. New Jersey: Lawrence Erlbaum Associates.

Longman Group Limited. (ed.) 1978. *Longman Dictionary of Contemporary English.* London: Longman Group Ltd.

Longman Group Limited. (ed.) 1979. *Longman Dictionary of English Idioms.* London: Longman Group Ltd.

Malgady, R. G. and M. Johnson. 1976. Modifiers in Metaphors: Effects of constituent phrase similarity on the interpretation of figurative sentences. *Journal of Psycholinguistic Research* 5: 43–52.

Martin, Samuel E. 1968. *New Korean –English Dictionary.* Seoul: Minjung-seokwan.

Matisoff, James A. 1991. Areal and Universal Dimensions of Grammaticalization in Lahu. *Approaches to Grammaticalization* Vol.2. ed. by Elizabeth C. Traugott and Bernd Heine, 383–453. Amsterdam: John Benjamins.

McCabe, Allyssa. 1983. Conceptual Similarity and the Quality of Metaphor in Isolated Sentences Versus Extended Contexts. *Journal of Psycholinguistic Research* 12.1: 41–68.

Nunberg, Geoffrey, Ivan A. Sag, and Thomas Wasow. 1994. Idioms. *Language* 70: 491–538.

Onions, C. T. (ed.) 1978. *The Shorter Oxford English Dictionary on historical principles.* 3rd. ed. Oxford: The Clarendon Press.

Ortony, Andrew, D. Schallert, R. Reynolds, and S. Antos. 1978. Interpreting Metaphors and Idioms: Some Effects of Context on Comprehension.

Journal of Verbal Learning and Verbal Behavior Vol. 17: 465−78.

Park, Yengcwun and Kyengpong Choy. (ed.) 1996. *Kwanyongesacen* [An Idiom Dictionary]. Seoul: Thayhaksa. (In Korean.)

Petrie, Hugh G. 1979. Metaphor and Learning. *Metaphor and Thought*, ed. by Andrew Ortony, 438−61. Cambridge: Cambridge University Press.

Prince, Alan and Paul Smolensky. 1993. *Optimality Theory: Constraint Interaction in Generative Grammar.* Rutgers University and University of Colorado, Boulder Ms. To appear, MIT Press.

Reddy, Michael J. 1979. The Conduit Metaphor. *Metaphor and Thought*, ed. by Andrew Ortony, 284−324. Cambridge: Cambridge University Press.

Renee, Edwards and Theodore Clevenger, Jr. 1990. The Effects of Schematic and Affective Processes on Metaphorical Invention. *Journal of Psycholinguistic Research* 19.2: 91−102.

Rhee, Seongha. 1998. *Munpephwauy Ihay* [Understanding of the Grammaticalization Theory]. Seoul: Hankwukmunhwasa. (In Korean.)

Rosch, Eleanor H. 1975. Cognitive Representations of Semantic Categories. *Journal of Experimental Psychology: General* 104: 192−233.

Saeed, John I. 1997. *Semantics.* Oxford: Blackwell.

Schraw, Gregory. 1995. Components of Metaphoric Processing. *Journal of Psycholinguistic Research* 24.1: 23−38.

Searle, John R. 1979. Metaphor. *Metaphor and Thought.* ed. by Andrew Ortony, 92−123. Cambridge: Cambridge University Press.

Seisaku, Kawakami. 1997. *An Introduction to Cognitive Linguistics.* Translated by Lee, kiwu, Cengay Lee, and Miyep Park. Seoul: Hankwukmunhwasa.

Shim, Jay−ki. 1985. Hankwuke Kwanyongphyohyenuy Hwayongloncekyenkwu. [A Pragmatic Study of Korean Idioms]. *Kwanakemunyenkwu* 11: 27−54. Seoul National University. (In Korean.)

Sticht, Thomas G. 1979. Educational Uses of Metaphor. *Metaphor and Thought*, ed. by Andrew Ortony, 474−85. Cambridge: Cambridge University Press.

Stock, Oliviero, Jon Slack, and Andrew Ortony. 1993. Building Castles in the Air: Some Computational and Theoretical Issues in Idiom Comprehension.

Idioms: Processing, Structure, and Interpretation, ed. by Cristina Cacciari and Patrizia Tabossi, 229−48. New Jersey: Lawrence Erlbaum Associates.

Sweetser, Eve E. 1990. *From Etymology to Pragmatics.* Cambridge: Cambridge University Press.

Swinney, D. and A. Cutler. 1979. The Access and Processing of Idiomatic Expressions. *Journal of Verbal Learning and Verbal Behavior* 18: 523−34.

Taylor, John R. 1989. *Linguistic Categorization: Prototypes in Linguistic Theory.* Oxford: Clarendon Press.

Traugott, Elizabeth C. and Ekkehard König. 1991. The Semantics−Pragmatics of Grammaticalization Revisited. *Approaches to Grammaticalization* Vol.1, ed. by Elizabeth C. Traugott and Bernd Heine, 190−218. Amsterdam: John Benjamins.

Turner, Mark and Gilles Fauconnier. 1998. Metaphor, Metonymy, and Binding. 10 pp. Online, Internet.

Ungerer, Friedrich and Hans−Jörg Schmid. 1996. *An Introduction to Cognitive Linguistics.* London & New York: Longman.

Wittgenstein, Ludwig. 1958. *Philosophical Investigations.* Translated by G. E. M. Anscobe. 2nd ed. Oxford: Blackwell.

Questionnaire for the Experiment in Chapter 4

Ⅰ. 다음 질문에 대하여 각 관용어의 뜻을 아는 대로 우리말로 쓰고, 문맥에 가장 부합된다고 생각하는 뜻을 선택해 주십시오. 또, 정도에 따라 나눈 등급에 표시해 주십시오.

[1] 관용어 *cook one's goose*

Betty **cooked her own goose** when she was rude to her employer.

1. 관용어 "cook her own goose"의 뜻은 무엇이라고 생각합니까?

2. What did Betty do when she cooked her own goose?
   a) She cooked a goose which she had.
   b) She was impolite.
   c) She made some food.
   d) She ruined the chances of success.

3. 본래 모르던 관용어입니까?

1	2	3	4
전혀 모름	알 듯 말 듯	대강 앎	완전히 앎

4. 본래 모르던 관용어인데, 함께 주어진 문맥 덕분에 뜻을 짐작하게 되었습니까?

그렇다   아니다

5. 이 문제의 경우에 문맥이 관용어의 뜻을 이해하는데 얼마나 도움이 된다고 생각합니까?

1	2	3	4
전혀 도움 안 됨	거의 도움 안 됨	약간 도움 됨	아주 많이 도움 됨

6. 이 문제의 경우에 개별 단어의 의미가 전체 관용어의 의미를 해석하는데 도움을 주었다면 어느 정도 도움이 되었다고 생각합니까?

1	2	3	4
전혀 도움 안 됨	거의 도움 안 됨	약간 도움 됨	아주 많이 도움 됨

[2] 관용어 *give up the ship*

Nick: "I don't know what to do about Henry, he continues to do so poorly in school."

Alice: "Don't **give up the ship**. I'm sure he'll do better once he improves his study habits."

1. 관용어 "give up the ship"의 뜻은 무엇이라고 생각합니까?

2. What does Alice suggest to Nick when she says, "Don't give
up the ship?"
   a) Nick must give the ship to Henry.
   b) Nick must stop saying to Henry.
   c) Nick must try to do something for Henry.
   d) Nick must abandon the ship.

3. 본래 모르던 관용어입니까?

1	2	3	4
전혀 모름	알 듯 말 듯	대강 앎	완전히 앎

4. 본래 모르던 관용어인데, 함께 주어진 문맥 덕분에 뜻을 짐작
하게 되었습니까?

그렇다   아니다

5. 이 문제의 경우에 문맥이 관용어의 뜻을 이해하는데 얼마나 도
움이 된다고 생각합니까?

1	2	3	4
전혀 도움 안 됨	거의 도움 안 됨	약간 도움 됨	아주 많이 도움 됨

6. 이 문제의 경우에 개별 단어의 의미가 전체 관용어의 의미를 해석
하는데 도움을 주었다면 어느 정도 도움이 되었다고 생각합니까?

1	2	3	4
전혀 도움 안 됨	거의 도움 안 됨	약간 도움 됨	아주 많이 도움 됨

[3] 관용어 *bite off more than one can chew*

Roger always sign up for the hardest courses on campus. On hiking trips, he always chooses the most dangerous trails even though he doesn't have enough hiking experience. He is the sort of person who always **bites off more than he can chew.**

1. 관용어 "bite off more than he can chew"의 뜻은 무엇이라고
생각합니까?

2. What action corresponds to biting off more than he can chew?
   a) To chew something that is bitten.
   b) To do something that is too difficult.
   c) To bite something that is too much.
   d) To attack someone.

3. 본래 모르던 관용어입니까?

1	2	3	4
전혀 모름	알 듯 말 듯	대강 앎	완전히 앎

4. 본래 모르던 관용어인데, 함께 주어진 문맥 덕분에 뜻을 짐작
   하게 되었습니까?

   그렇다   아니다

5. 이 문제의 경우에 문맥이 관용어의 뜻을 이해하는데 얼마나 도
   움이 된다고 생각합니까?

   1   2   3   4
전혀 도움 안 됨   거의 도움 안 됨   약간 도움 됨   아주 많이 도움 됨

6. 이 문제의 경우에 개별 단어의 의미가 전체 관용어의 의미를 해석
   하는데 도움을 주었다면 어느 정도 도움이 되었다고 생각합니까?

   1   2   3   4
전혀 도움 안 됨   거의 도움 안 됨   약간 도움 됨   아주 많이 도움 됨

[4] 관용어 *break the ice*

A little boy named Paul moved to another town, so he had to change school. His mother suggested that he should try and get to know his new schoolmates. Once at school he lent them his crayons and that helped to **break the ice**.

1. 관용어 "break the ice"의 뜻은 무엇이라고 생각합니까?

2. What did Paul do when he broke the ice?

   a) He made friends with his schoolmates.

   b) He broke a piece of ice.

   c) He told his mom everything.

   d) He did something dangerous.

3. 본래 모르던 관용어입니까?

1	2	3	4
전혀 모름	알 듯 말 듯	대강 앎	완전히 앎

4. 본래 모르던 관용어인데, 함께 주어진 문맥 덕분에 뜻을 짐작하게 되었습니까?

       그렇다   아니다

5. 이 문제의 경우에 문맥이 관용어의 뜻을 이해하는데 얼마나 도움이 된다고 생각합니까?

1	2	3	4
전혀 도움 안 됨	거의 도움 안 됨	약간 도움 됨	아주 많이 도움 됨

6. 이 문제의 경우에 개별 단어의 의미가 전체 관용어의 의미를 해석하는데 도움을 주었다면 어느 정도 도움이 되었다고 생각합니까?

1	2	3	4
전혀 도움 안 됨	거의 도움 안 됨	약간 도움 됨	아주 많이 도움 됨

[5] 관용어 *pull a fast one*

Some shopkeepers often try to **pull a fast one** by selling low quality goods at high prices.

1. 관용어 "pull a fast one"의 뜻은 무엇이라고 생각합니까?

2. What do some shopkeepers do by pulling a fast one?
    a) They often draw something to another place.
    b) They often deceive people who will buy something.
    c) They often move carts with force.
    d) They often sell goods quickly.

3. 본래 모르던 관용어입니까?

1	2	3	4
전혀 모름	알 듯 말 듯	대강 앎	완전히 앎

4. 본래 모르던 관용어인데, 함께 주어진 문맥 덕분에 뜻을 짐작 하게 되었습니까?

그렇다   아니다

5. 이 문제의 경우에 문맥이 관용어의 뜻을 이해하는데 얼마나 도움이 된다고 생각합니까?

1	2	3	4
전혀 도움 안 됨	거의 도움 안 됨	약간 도움 됨	아주 많이 도움 됨

6. 이 문제의 경우에 개별 단어의 의미가 전체 관용어의 의미를 해석하는데 도움을 주었다면 어느 정도 도움이 되었다고 생각합니까?

1	2	3	4
전혀 도움 안 됨	거의 도움 안 됨	약간 도움 됨	아주 많이 도움 됨

[6] 관용어 *on pins and needles*

Jack was on pins and needles while he was answering my questions—he was clearly worried that I would find out something that he didn't want me to know.

1. 관용어 "on pins and needles"의 뜻은 무엇이라고 생각합니까?

2. What is Jack's state or attitude?
   a) He was sitting on something sharp.
   b) He was eager to do something.
   c) He was anxious and uneasy.
   d) He was doing something with pins and needles.

3. 본래 모르던 관용어입니까?

1	2	3	4
전혀 모름	알 듯 말 듯	대강 앎	완전히 앎

4. 본래 모르던 관용어인데, 함께 주어진 문맥 덕분에 뜻을 짐작
   하게 되었습니까?

그렇다   아니다

5. 이 문제의 경우에 문맥이 관용어의 뜻을 이해하는데 얼마나 도
   움이 된다고 생각합니까?

1	2	3	4
전혀 도움 안 됨	거의 도움 안 됨	약간 도움 됨	아주 많이 도움 됨

6. 이 문제의 경우에 개별 단어의 의미가 전체 관용어의 의미를 해석
   하는데 도움을 주었다면 어느 정도 도움이 되었다고 생각합니까?

1	2	3	4
전혀 도움 안 됨	거의 도움 안 됨	약간 도움 됨	아주 많이 도움 됨

[7] 관용어 *carry coals to Newcastle*

It would be like **carrying coals to Newcastle** if another bank
opened in this street: there are three banks here now.

1. 관용어 "carrying coals to Newcastle"의 뜻은 무엇이라고 생각
   합니까?

2. What action corresponds to carrying coals to Newcastle?

   a) To establish some institutions.

   b) To supply some fuels.

   c) To do something that is completely unnecessary.

   d) To carry something to a certain place.

3. 본래 모르던 관용어입니까?

1	2	3	4
전혀 모름	알 듯 말 듯	대강 앎	완전히 앎

4. 본래 모르던 관용어인데, 함께 주어진 문맥 덕분에 뜻을 짐작
   하게 되었습니까?

   그렇다   아니다

5. 이 문제의 경우에 문맥이 관용어의 뜻을 이해하는데 얼마나 도
   움이 된다고 생각합니까?

1	2	3	4
전혀 도움 안 됨	거의 도움 안 됨	약간 도움 됨	아주 많이 도움 됨

6. 이 문제의 경우에 개별 단어의 의미가 전체 관용어의 의미를 해석하는데 도움을 주었다면 어느 정도 도움이 되었다고 생각합니까?

1	2	3	4
전혀 도움 안 됨	거의 도움 안 됨	약간 도움 됨	아주 많이 도움 됨

[8] 관용어 *face the music*

Peter hitchhiked to Dover and took a day trip to France. But his continental fling ended when he could not pay for his meal. Now he is on the way back to *Bristol—to **face the music**.
* Bristol is a port city on the southwestern part of England.

1. 관용어 "face the music"의 뜻은 무엇이라고 생각합니까?

2. What do you think Peter should do when he faced the music?
   a) He should play the music.
   b) He should accept the difficulties.
   c) He should go home.
   d) He should meet musicians.

3. 본래 모르던 관용어입니까?

1	2	3	4
전혀 모름	알 듯 말 듯	대강 앎	완전히 앎

4. 본래 모르던 관용어인데, 함께 주어진 문맥 덕분에 뜻을 짐작하게 되었습니까?

그렇다   아니다

5. 이 문제의 경우에 문맥이 관용어의 뜻을 이해하는데 얼마나 도움이 된다고 생각합니까?

1   2   3   4
전혀 도움 안 됨   거의 도움 안 됨   약간 도움 됨   아주 많이 도움 됨

6. 이 문제의 경우에 개별 단어의 의미가 전체 관용어의 의미를 해석하는데 도움을 주었다면 어느 정도 도움이 되었다고 생각합니까?

1   2   3   4
전혀 도움 안 됨   거의 도움 안 됨   약간 도움 됨   아주 많이 도움 됨

[9] 관용어 *beat around the bush*

Tell me the truth: don't **beat around the bush**!

1. 관용어 "beat around the bush"의 뜻은 무엇이라고 생각합니까?

2. What should you do in order not to beat around the bush?
   a) I should speak something frankly.
   b) I should delay talking about something.
   c) I should say what I want to have.

d) I should avoid what I want to say.

3. 본래 모르던 관용어입니까?

1	2	3	4
전혀 모름	알 듯 말 듯	대강 앎	완전히 앎

4. 본래 모르던 관용어인데, 함께 주어진 문맥 덕분에 뜻을 짐작하게 되었습니까?

그렇다   아니다

5. 이 문제의 경우에 문맥이 관용어의 뜻을 이해하는데 얼마나 도움이 된다고 생각합니까?

1	2	3	4
전혀 도움 안 됨	거의 도움 안 됨	약간 도움 됨	아주 많이 도움 됨

6. 이 문제의 경우에 개별 단어의 의미가 전체 관용어의 의미를 해석하는데 도움을 주었다면 어느 정도 도움이 되었다고 생각합니까?

1	2	3	4
전혀 도움 안 됨	거의 도움 안 됨	약간 도움 됨	아주 많이 도움 됨

II. 다음 관용어들을 비슷한 개념을 나타낸다고 생각되는 것끼리 두 부류로 나누어 group 1과 group 2에 그 번호를 써 주십시오. 왜 그렇게 나누었는지 각 관용어마다 간단히 그 이유를 써 주십시오. 자신이 받은 느낌을 솔직히 써 주십시오. 분명하지 않더라도 괜찮고 약간의 느낌이라도 좋습니다. 보기를 보고 그와 같이 해 주십시오.

[보기]

1) hit the ceiling   2) lose one's cool   3) lay down the law
4) let off steam   5) crack the whip   6) call the shots
7) foam at the mouth   8) wear the pants   9) go crazy

위의 관용어들을 두 부류로 나눈다면 아래와 같이 됩니다.

<group 1> 모두 화(ANGER)에 관한 관용어

   1) hit the ceiling: 화가 머리끝까지 나서 천장을 칠 정도이므로.

   2) lose one's cool: 화가 나서 이성을 잃을 정도이므로.

   4) let off steam: 화(steam)를 발산하는 것이므로.

   7) foam at the mouth: 화가 나서 입에 거품을 물 정도이므로.

   9) go crazy: 화가 나서 미칠 지경이므로.

<group 2> 권위(AUTHORITY)나 통제(CONTROL)의 의미가 담긴 관용어

   3) lay down the law: law를 세우는 것이므로.

   5) crack the whip: 채찍을 치는 것이므로.

   6) call the shots: control events의 뜻. shots에서 추측할 수 있다.

   8) wear the pants: '결혼생활에서 주도권을 쥐다'의 뜻이므로.

잘 모를 경우에는 어떤 단어 때문에 또는 어떤 느낌 때문이라고
만 언급해도 됩니다.

[문제]

1) keep it under one's hat   2) hold one's tongue   3) button one's lips
4) let the cat out of the bag 5) loose lips   6) spill the beans
7) blow the lid off   8) keep in the dark   9) blow the whistle

<group 1>

<group 2>

Ⅲ. 다음 관용어들의 뜻을 쓰고 아는 정도에 따라 표시해 주십시오. 틀려도 좋으니 자신이 생각한 뜻을 써 주십시오. 왜 그런 뜻이라고 생각했는지 단서가 있다면 써 주십시오.

1. blue를 포함하는 관용어

	뜻 쓰기	아는 정도 표시			
		전혀 모름	알 듯 말 듯	약간 앎	완전히 앎
1) true blue		1	2	3	4
2) blue chip		1	2	3	4
3) blue Monday		1	2	3	4
4) blue law		1	2	3	4
5) blue collar		1	2	3	4
6) blue blood		1	2	3	4

2. black을 포함하는 관용어

	뜻 쓰기	아는 정도 표시			
		전혀 모름	알 듯 말 듯	약간 앎	완전히 앎
1) be in the black		1	2	3	4
2) black art		1	2	3	4
3) black magic		1	2	3	4
4) black list		1	2	3	4
5) black Friday		1	2	3	4
6) black market		1	2	3	4
7) black sheep		1	2	3	4
8) black look		1	2	3	4
9) Black Law		1	2	3	4
10) black-letter day		1	2	3	4

3. white를 포함하는 관용어

	뜻 쓰기	아는 정도 표시			
		전혀 모름	알 듯 말 듯	약간 앎	완전히 앎
1) turn white		1	2	3	4
2) white lie		1	2	3	4
3) white-handed		1	2	3	4
4) white magic		1	2	3	4
5) a white flag		1	2	3	4
6) white collar		1	2	3	4
7) white dress		1	2	3	4
8) white remark		1	2	3	4

4. red를 포함하는 관용어

	뜻 쓰기	아는 정도 표시			
		전혀 모름	알 듯 말 듯	약간 앎	완전히 앎
1) turn red		1	2	3	4
2) red heat		1	2	3	4
3) see red		1	2	3	4
4) red light		1	2	3	4
5) red carpet		1	2	3	4
6) Red Cross		1	2	3	4
7) be in the red		1	2	3	4
8) red-letter day		1	2	3	4
9) red-handed		1	2	3	4
10) red hunting		1	2	3	4
11) red herring		1	2	3	4
12) red tape		1	2	3	4
13) red guy		1	2	3	4
14) red lie		1	2	3	4

5. yellow를 포함하는 관용어

	뜻 쓰기	아는 정도 표시			
		전혀 모름	알 듯 말 듯	약간 앎	완전히 앎
1) too yellow to fight		1	2	3	4
2) yellow press		1	2	3	4
3) yellow fever		1	2	3	4
4) yellow race		1	2	3	4
5) yellow person		1	2	3	4
6) someone's future is yellow		1	2	3	4

6. green을 포함하는 관용어

	뜻 쓰기	아는 정도 표시			
		전혀 모름	알 듯 말 듯	약간 앎	완전히 앎
1) green-eyed		1	2	3	4
2) green light		1	2	3	4
3) green memory		1	2	3	4
4) a green hand		1	2	3	4

다음과 같은 색채어를 들을 때 드는 느낌을 생각나는 순서대로 모두 적어 주십시오.

1. 검정 혹은 검은색

2. 하양 또는 흰색

3. 빨강 또는 빨간색

4. 파랑 또는 파란색

5. 푸른색

6. 노랑 또는 노란색

7. 초　록

8. 녹　색

1. Transparent Idioms(Explanation Group=Experiment Group)

	degree of correct answering	degree of correct answering among examples	degree of knowing (1: not know −4: know completely)	degree of feeling that context is helpful	contributing degree of context (1 −4)	contributing degree of constituent meaning (1 −4)
1. break the ice	0.6	0.96	1.52	0.8	3.52	3.04
2. bite off more than one can chew	0.72	0.96	1.375	0.84	3.375	3.04
3. on pins and needles	0.44	0.8	1.36	0.84	3.16	2.64
average	0.586667	0.906667	1.418333	0.826667	3.3516667	2.907222
standard deviation	0.141475	0.092376	0.088365	0.023094	0.181131	0.231423

2. Transparent Idioms(No Explanation Group=Control Group)

	degree of correct answering	degree of correct answering among examples	degree of knowing (1: not know, −4: know completely)	degree of feeling that context is helpful	contributing degree of context (1 −4)	contributing degree of constituent meaning (1 −4)
1. break the ice	0.5	0.86	1.398182	0.863636	3.181818	2.590909
2. bite off more than one can chew	0.59	0.95	1.363636	0.95	3.409091	2.954545
3. on pins and needles	0.41	0.77	1.409091	0.77	3.136364	2.863636
average	0.5	0.86	1.390303	0.861212	3.242424	2.80303
standard deviation	0.09	0.09	0.02373	0.090024	0.146116	0.189242

3. The Average of the Experiment Group and the Control Group

	degree of correct answering	degree of correct answering among examples	degree of knowing (1: not know, −4: know completely)	degree of feeling that context is helpful	contributing degree of context (1 −4)	contributing degree of constituent meaning (1 −4)
Experiment Group	0.586667	0.906667	1.1418883	0.826667	3.351667	2.907222
Control Group	0.5	0.86	1.390303	0.861212	3.242424	2.80303
Average	0.543334	0.883334	1.266068	0.84394	3.297046	2.855126

4. Less Transparent Idioms(Experiment Group)

	degree of correct answering	degree of correct answering among examples	degree of knowing (1: not know, −4: know completely)	degree of feeling that context is helpful	contributing degree of context (1−4)	contributing degree of constituent meaning (1−4)
1. give up the ship	0.52	0.84	1.48	0.96	3.52	2.96
2. carry coals to New Castle	0.36	0.52	1.2	0.76	3	2.6
3. beat around the bush	0.48	0.76	1.8	0.68	3.08	2.52
average	0.453333	0.706667	1.493333	0.8	3.2	2.693333
standard deviation	0.083267	0.166533	0.300222	0.144222	0.28	0.234379

5. Less Transparent Idioms(Control Group)

	degree of correct answering	degree of correct answering among examples	degree of knowing (1: not know, −4: know completely)	degree of feeling that context is helpful	contributing degree of context (1 −4)	contributing degree of constituent meaning (1 −4)
1. give up the ship	0.545454	0.81818	1.5	0.954545	3.31818	2.72727
2. carry coals to New Castle	0.22727	0.181818	1.136364	0.772727	3.045455	2.272727
3. beat around the bush	0.454545	0.863636	1.681818	0.909	3.318182	2.954545
average	0.40909	0.621211	1.439394	0.878757	3.227272	2.651514
standard deviation	0.16389	0.381204	0.277732	0.094607	0.157458	0.347164

6. The Average of the Experiment Group and the Control Group

	degree of correct answering	degree of correct answering among examples	degree of knowing (1: not know, −4: know completely)	degree of feeling that context is helpful	contributing degree of context (1 −4)	contributing degree of constituent meaning (1 −4)
Experiment Group	0.453333	0.706667	1.493333	0.8	3.2	2.693333
Control Group	0.40909	0.621211	1.439394	0.878757	3.227272	2.651514
Average	0.431212	0.663939	1.466364	0.839379	3.213636	2.672424

7. Opaque Idioms(Experiment Group)

	degree of correct answering	degree of correct answering among examples	degree of knowing (1: not know, -4: know completely)	degree of feeling that context is helpful	contributing degree of context $(1-4)$	contributing degree of constituent meaning $(1-4)$
1. cook one's goose	0.09	0.363636	1.318182	0.772727	3.045455	2
2. pull a fast one	0.09	0.636363	1.090909	0.772727	2.818182	2.272727
3. face the music	0.136363	0.40909	1.181818	0.545454	2.545455	2.090909
average	0.105454	0.469696	1.19697	0.696969	2.803031	2.121212
standard deviation	0.026768	0.146116	0.114392	0.131216	0.250344	0.138866

8. The Average of the Experiment Group and the Control Group

	degree of correct answering	degree of correct answering among examples	degree of knowing (1: not know, -4: know completely)	degree of feeling that context is helpful	contributing degree of context $(1-4)$	contributing degree of constituent meaning $(1-4)$
Experiment Group	0.093333	0.36	1.213333	0.733333	2.933333	2.226667
Control Group	0.105454	0.469696	1.19697	0.696969	2.803031	2.121212
Average	0.099394	0.414848	1.205152	0.715151	2.868182	2.17394

• 저자 •

박경선   •약 력•
1960년 서울 출생.
2001년 한국외국어대학교 영어과에서 박사학위 받음.
한국외국어대학교 서양학대학 영어과 대우교수를 거쳐서
현재 미국 미시간주 앤아버시에 체류 중.

•주요논저•
「영어와 한국어의 색채어와 신체어에 나타나는 개념적 은유」
「영어의 일부 서법조동사의 문법화에 관하여」
「영어 완료형의 be / have 변이형에 관하여」
외 다수

A Cognitive Linguistic Approach to English Idioms
From a Pedagogical Perspective

• 초판 인쇄	2007년 11월 30일
• 초판 발행	2007년 11월 30일
• 지 은 이	박경선
• 펴 낸 이	채종준
• 펴 낸 곳	한국학술정보㈜
	경기도 파주시 교하읍 문발리 513-5
	파주출판문화정보산업단지
	전화 031) 908-3181(대표) · 팩스 031) 908-3189
	홈페이지 http://www.kstudy.com
	e-mail(출판사업부) publish@kstudy.com
• 등 록	제일산-115호(2000. 6. 19)
• 가 격	22,000원

ISBN   978-89-534-7657-8 93840 (Paper Book)
        978-89-534-7658-5 98840 (e-Book)